T0166371

CANDYASS

CANDYASS

Nick Comilla

Arsenal Pulp Press
Vancouver

CANDYASS
Copyright © 2016 by Nick Comilla

All rights reserved. No part of this book may be reproduced in any part by any means—graphic, electronic, or mechanical—without the prior written permission of the publisher, except by a reviewer, who may use brief excerpts in a review, or in the case of photocopying in Canada, a license from Access Copyright.

ARSENAL PULP PRESS
Suite 202 – 211 East Georgia St.
Vancouver, BC V6A 1Z6
Canada
arsenalpulp.com

This is a work of fiction. Any resemblance of characters to persons either living or deceased is purely coincidental.

Cover photograph by Matt Lambert
Cover and text design by Oliver McPartlin
Edited by Susan Safyan

Printed and bound in Canada

Library and Archives Canada Cataloguing in Publication:
Comilla, Nick, 1988-, author
    Candyass / Nick Comilla.

Issued in print and electronic formats.
ISBN 978-1-55152-664-5 (paperback).—ISBN 978-1-55152-665-2 (html)

    I. Title.

PS3603.O5517C36 2016   813'.6   C2016-905526-4
                                    C2016-905527-2

"I've known every young man of means."
—Arthur Rimbaud, "Bad Blood"

PART 1
freshmen

This is what it's like: I never know what day of the week it is. I get so down I drift through and feel up. We get so high we forget it wears off. The clothes are tight to our skin like tattoos, but they slip off effortlessly. Our wrists have been stamped so many times, there's a shadow on the skin. Shadows under our eyes. I get so used to seeing people in flashing lights—red, blue, black, white, purple; their eyes all shimmer in rays of amber—that when people aren't flashing and changing colours, that's when my eyes have to adjust. They're almost always seventeen with a fake ID and a huge ego, or eighteen or nineteen. I kiss them with such convincing passion that they have no idea how turned off I am and why I don't ask them to come back home with me. But it wasn't always like that.

*

One night, I decided, this was it. I got dressed in tight jeans and a bright red tank top. It was August. The summer was nearly over. I cruised the streets, knowing no one. I wasn't sure how all of this was supposed to work. The streets were flooded with people, but what was I supposed to do—just go up to someone and say, *Hey, do you want to fuck?* It was hard to meet people, and I didn't know how to flirt. I felt desire but didn't know how to express it. I wandered into a club that I had heard about. On the outside, it looked like a giant old post office, almost Romanesque. Once inside, the man at the coat check gave me a dirty look and took my five dollars. I walked past a doorway that had black leather straps hanging down, and into the club. Inside, I could hardly see. It smelled like chlorine. There was hard-core gay porn playing on the screens and a shirtless, hairy bartender. I wandered around, avoiding the decorative metal chains that hung down all over the place. I would later come to realize that it was early, eleven p.m., and so hardly anyone was there. I looked up into the DJ booth and saw a boy with headphones on and black hair like mine. I wanted my opposite, a blond, but at least he was my age. I walked over to the booth and stood beneath it, smiling. I waved. He waved.

Later that night, when he was done with his DJ set, we went back to his apartment near the Frontenac Metro station, a part of the city I had never been to before, the east end, where Anglophone boys don't normally go. He was wearing blue jeans and a white button down T-shirt—how boring—though I found him attractive enough. In high school, I'd wanted to fall in love, lose my virginity in some kind of passionate relationship. But at this point, I just wanted to do it. I needed to fuck something. Horniness was seeping from my pores. I couldn't think about anything else. Losing your virginity in a one-night stand isn't such a big deal, I decided. It's sort of a classic homosexual thing to do. Sure, it would have been nice if it was special, but it was better than nothing: it showed you that, well, here it is, this is sex, in its most basic form.

His apartment was nicely furnished, like a wealthy person's apartment. How could a guy my own age afford all of this? Impossible. We lay down on his bed, which was in the living room.

"Um, I've never done this before," I told him, nervous and excited.

"It's okay," he said. "Just do what I say."

I lay on top of him, making out. Simple enough, I thought. Then he rolled over, unbuttoned my pants, and began to blow me. What I was most curious about, though, was licking his ass. How could you possibly be any closer to another guy other than licking his ass? There is nothing more personal. On one hand, you're giving pleasure, so it's active, but on the other hand, it's an act of worship, so it's oddly passive. Plus, you're getting his pheromones all over your face. It is basically spiritual. Rimming is an act of everything coming full circle.

"Um ... could I like ... lick your butt, dude?" I asked him.

He smiled and rolled over onto his stomach. I went at it. It was everything I thought it would be. I have arrived, I thought. I was shocked at how ass really had no taste for something that always smelled so particular. I gave him what was probably the most amateur rim job he'd ever received, just lapping my tongue up and down on his asshole like a dog. I didn't care. I was in bliss. But then came the actual sex part. He rolled over with his legs wrapped around me, my chest pressed against his. With his hips, he started to pull me in. The tip of my cock pressed into him before I realized it. I paused and put a condom on, convinced that if I ever had gay sex without a condom I'd get AIDS. Then I did it, the thing I had been waiting so many years to do. I fucked him, thinking it would be a transgressive feeling, but it wasn't. With lube on, I just bounced in and out of him, switching positions, my chest and stomach smashing into his back. I tried to fuck him like I had seen in porn, but he was even looser than any guy I saw in porn.

I fucked him until he finished, and I watched him cum. And then that was it. I spent the night there and gave him a kiss on the forehead in the morning, my habit of unwarranted affection already developing. Overall, I felt glad. He'd taken a part of me that I'd been trying to get rid of for years. Virginity was gone, and in her place, I imagined, came the muses, the goddesses of inspiration, music, and passion. I just had to dump that bitch virginity into a garbage can first. I walked out of his apartment that morning a brand-new boy, a non-virgin. I stumbled around the east end with a hangover and a headache, occasionally wafting the scent of sex on my fingers in front of my face. That makes me happy, I thought. Life isn't so bad after all.

Eventually I found the Metro station and took it home, back to the Plateau. I would fall asleep in the middle of the day when I didn't have any classes and have wildly lucid dreams. I decided I didn't care if I ever saw him again—that wasn't the goal. The goal was to become impure, to finally lose the sense of innocence that I loathed. I got tested the next day, freaking out about the tip, the tip. I'd stuck the tip in. Worried sick about the tip. I got so sick from worrying that I thought the sick feeling was AIDS. I paid eighty dollars for an HIV test, which should have been free, and endured dirty looks from the doctor. The results came back negative. I took a handful of condoms and left the office.

*

I was so clueless when I first moved to Montreal; I knew nothing, no one. The first really beautiful boy I met was Xavier. I met him on the Internet. I was stunned—he seemed remarkably normal, like the guys I'd known on soccer teams. Growing up, I'd spent so much time feeling alienated, partially for being gay, that somehow, subconsciously, I got it in my mind that all gay boys were awkward. This was a caricature that I had come to know from mass culture, which is, of course, run and ruined by heterosexuals. What I started to discover is that that was a myth:

We are, largely, just boys and men who want to fuck and love other boys and men. There was no single kind of homosexual. Perhaps there were multiple kinds of homosexualities. I had convinced myself in high school that the youthful masculine ideal I desired was unattainable because gay men were never like that, like the straight boys I lusted after in vain. But I had gone, almost overnight, from a culture where gay people were depicted as awkward, depressed, overweight, or excessively flamboyant, to a place where young gay men were known for their artistic talent and good looks. There was a higher degree of *outness* in Montreal, outness being a thing that expands the scope of homosexuals.

Xavier took me to bars and clubs. I knew from the start that we had little in common, but that face of his ...

"We'll go to Drugstore first, and then to Parking," he told me.

"Okay, but why do you need to go to the drugstore?" I asked him.

"No," he replied, laughing. "I don't need to go to the drugstore. Drugstore is a bar, kind of a lesbian bar."

"Oh, okay. And then we'll find parking after that?"

"Oh god, you're so cute. No, Parking is the name of a club."

Xavier took me out and showed me the scene. Or at least, his scene. But I soon realized that Xavier was a prude and possibly a virgin, which just made all the guys go even crazier. All I could think about was how tight his ass must be.

That summer, I caught the first glimpse of the splinters within gay culture, the reactions to liberation. We'd once been excited about being able to fuck freely, and now we were so bored that some of us had retreated into suburban sexuality. Xavier was free to fuck for a long time, so maybe the only thrill for him was to be free to decide who he fucked and when. I was his summer friend, and he was my summer crush. I was usually buzzed if not outright drunk—I had to be in order to handle all of those hundreds of people, the pounding music, the energy. A friend of Xavier's once looked at me and said, "You just moved here from the States in early July, and you're eighteen with no job, nothing to do until school starts?" He said it seemed so random, but I didn't understand that it was strange for someone to move to Montreal from so far away. It's a big city, sure, but because it was on the other side of the US border, most Americans didn't consider moving there.

One weekday, Xavier and his friend Chris and I hung out together. I came to realize that was special, because the people I hung out with in Montreal had real friends and "night friends." We were young and didn't know how to integrate the two. Normally, during the weekdays, I was quite lost, listless, living in a city where I didn't speak the language. I'd spend my days wandering around alone. Even though I knew it probably wouldn't last, I took up Xavier's initiation at actual, daytime friendship. We drove into the suburb Xavier was from—a suburb I'd later come to think of as the suburb of love—and spent the evening at his house. We walked around, climbed trees, had dinner with his parents. It was weird trying to be normal and hang out with them outside of a club setting. Later on, he took us to a neighbourhood friend's house, and we watched him jump on their trampoline. So high. Chris and I looked at each other, smiling, both thinking the same thing, sharing this moment of desire. We both wanted him, but no one could have him. Neither of us were there for friendship.

I grew to resent Xavier. The last time we went out together to a club, I drunkenly told him, "I think this is bullshit! This is so fake, all of this. This is not what I'm about. I like rock music." I left him at the club. I was trying to convince myself that I hadn't changed at all. I didn't know exactly what the problem was, but I felt a massive reaction to what I deemed as vapid, shallow gay-club culture. Still, I would always come back, and there would be new boys, new mythologies, and like so many others before him, Xavier was long gone.

*

While I was gradually settling in, I started to go to all sorts of parties and become friends, night friends, with different people. I had never cared much for electronic music before I moved to Montreal, but it started to grow on me. What had once seemed like mindless repetition became a kind of spiritual, syncopated trance, a frequency wave. There were all kinds of parties, but I preferred the more dank, dark, industrial variety.

I was on a search for my twin half. The more colourful, pop-oriented places had beautiful boys, but little substance. The dark, industrial gigs had the characters, the weirdo brethren whom I longed for. The rooms were always purposefully dark, and all I could smell was beer and boy sweat, and I loved it. It smelled like punk rock. Harsh, intense, pounding electro would flow from the speakers. One track in particular would play at every party, the loop encapsulating the night— asexual, trisexual, transsexual, bisexual—repeated over and over again. A lesbian acquaintance introduced me to a pixie fairy boy, very short, much shorter than me, at six-foot-one. He looked young, but I could tell that this, like so much else, was an illusion. He told me that he was twenty-six, and I told him I was eighteen; the age difference seemed too much and was a turn-off to both of us, so we went our separate ways. My search continued: I needed to know the world.

*

It's Friday night, and I'm at one of the more underground parties. The looming alternative to the gay village, a strange new phenomenon, at least to me and people my age. People tend to talk a lot of shit about the gay village in these circles. Apparently, being free is boring. They want a return to secrecy, to feeling deviant, to a past we can't experience. It's a nostalgia for oppression, born out of privilege. What was once liberation has warped into assimilation. Now there is "gay," and there is "queer." I think it's a lot of bullshit, though—we are mostly just gay kids alienated from the larger gay culture, from consumerism, conformity, and a very narrow view of what being gay can include.

Others disagree, giving up on the term gay altogether and adopting, partially due to their own overly academic lives, the queer identity. Queer is the new cool. At the end of the day, we are still mostly just guys fucking other guys, with some gender non-conformity thrown into the mix and an awareness of class and privilege—smart fags—and now you have a new scene, a scene whose nose could still sniff the coke off your key, but then turn right back around and point it high up in the air, scoffing at you ... I am ambivalent about the whole thing and sympathize with both sides. On one hand, I did feel that the village was stripped of the punk attitude I long for. I think of boys like Xavier, who probably only feel their oppression in very minute ways, so their desire never really conflicts with their existence.

But I also recognize that the village itself—and anything like it—is a result of a radical struggle inherently tied to class and language. But people seem to forget that. They forget that, to young queers who've just moved to Montreal, the village is the first place where they can be surrounded by other people like them. I wonder how something so inherently political could be condemned as depoliticized.

Michael, a guy I've seen around school a few times, is at the party tonight. We exchange glances. He has an asymmetrical haircut, glasses, tight black jeans with a key ring on one loop, plugs stretching his ears, and a tight black shirt that says *LIMP WRIST* on it, a band I used to listen to in high school. We chat a little bit about school, and he ends up asking me if he can crash at my place for the night, since he lives so far away, in the southwest part of the city. This is getting to be a common occurrence—people staying with random strangers they've just met, even if not explicitly for sexual purposes. Usually it works out, but can sometimes be awkward. Taxis are expensive, and the Metro shuts down after 1:30—that's our excuse, and we're sticking to it, but really, we're probably just lonely. So I let him stay with me. A few weeks later, he tells me that a room has opened up in his house—a communal queer living situation, he calls it—in a working-class neighbourhood. For only $250 a month, it's a lot cheaper than my current room, which is $400 a month, so a few weeks later, I move in.

*

One night, before moving in with Michael and his lesbian roommate Alice, I had what I can understand only as my first out-of-body experience or astral projection. A devout atheist, I had read too much Camus and Sartre when I was younger, so I didn't know what to make of the experience at first. The lucid dreams I could handle, but this was something else entirely. I was lying in bed, and my mind drifted into a trance-like meditation state, but I still retained consciousness, I was still awake. Trying to stay calm as I lay there, I felt my body gradually become numb, asleep. Suddenly I heard a loud whooshing noise, like I was being sucked through a kind of vortex. I could feel vibrations all around me. When it was over, I could still feel the pulse of the vibrations. I decided to try to sit up, but instead my body stayed still while I lifted up out it. I looked around the room, then back down at my body, overcome with an amazing feeling of freedom. Taking a breath, it felt like I had been underwater my entire life, and that that was the first real breath I ever took.

Everything seemed more or less the same as I looked around my room, just a little different in terms of colours, more radiant, pulsating. I floated out into the hallway, toward the front door, and contemplated opening it and seeing what else was out there. I knew I could not have been dreaming because everything was just too real—plus I had a full awareness of my body back in my room. My hand on the doorknob, I was overcome with doubt and fear about what would happen if I opened the door. As soon as those emotions crossed my mind, I was back inside my own physical body, in a daze. Nothing has ever been the same since.

*

Summertime after first year. I'm back in Pennsylvania, visiting the bumfuck, white-trash, redneck town I grew up in. Bored as hell—a feeling I almost forgot. I just finished a brief fling with a boy named Samuel. We would jerk off together and he would sit on my face and he was blond and eighteen and that was it. I asked him if he liked me and he told me he appreciated me. Which meant no. I wrote some poems about it. I keep going with cuter and cuter boys and it's strange to me because I never thought I was particularly attractive, but maybe I'm in bloom too or maybe I was this whole time and I felt so bad about myself before that I didn't realize it. Because now everything has changed and I can get almost anyone I want.

I'm on my laptop and I randomly sign into AIM, a chat program we used during high school. There is a boy online named Nathan who broke my heart in high school, kind of. He lived a couple towns over, about a forty-five-minute drive away, and we would chat online sometimes. I was out by then, and I had guessed he was gay from his Myspace pics. I'm not sure how I could tell, there was nothing overt about it, just something in his eyes, this slight kind of brightness. I asked him out back then but he turned me down, which crushed me, because he was my only shot. I was devastated, of course: I pictured myself going to prom with him, thinking maybe life won't be so bad, like, maybe I'll move to Pittsburgh or something and live this normal life and be in a normal relationship. But no. He told me once that I didn't look very "classy." He was a preppie-looking boy, and I was a punky queer stoner boy, I guess.

I message him and say hi, explain that I'm in town visiting from college. I tell him how we used to talk and that he was kind of a jerk. He doesn't remember me, or at least pretends not to. We exchange some photos, and he's suddenly very interested in meeting, immediately. Later that day, he drives into town while I have the house to myself. We go for a ride, just driving around this little town, making awkward conversation. We drive past a group of high school kids who stare at us. Nathan is sixteen; he's also a high school kid. Sixteen. Sixteen. Sweet sixteen. I'm nineteen, so it's not that big of a difference, but still. It's June, the month of youth. The stars are on my side. He is beautiful but stupid, has nothing interesting to say. But he has a boyish face, bright brown eyes, short dirty-blond hair. Khaki pants. He's from a town named Du Bois, which is pronounced Do Boys.

We go through a car wash. The windows are rolled up, and for an extended instant we are completely alone under the darkness of the flaps and brushes. I turn to him. "I think it would be kind of fun to make out while going through a car wash," I suggest. "Sure," he says, to my surprise. So I lean over while the car is being pulled along the conveyor belt and kiss him as hard as I wanted to kiss him back in high school. His spit tastes like sugarcane. The inside of his lips are like a peach. The car comes out sparkling clean, shining a brilliant blood red, and he keeps driving. We're on a back road, surrounded by forest. I have a weakness for rural boys. I unzip his pants, pull out his cock. It's rock fucking hard and surprisingly huge. "Wow," I say. He smiles, boyishly coy. I put my mouth on it, and it smells amazing. There is a sweetness that only the genitals of younger guys possess, I'm sure of it. I can't prove it, but you'll just have to take my word for it. It just smells like pure fucking pristine skin. We drive around while I suck on him, his hand pushing down on my head.

We go back to the house that I grew up in, now empty. Up to my high school bedroom, where I had long since given up hope of ever having sex. I feel like I am going through some kind of rebirth: I left, I returned, and now I shall conquer. We go into the room, and I close the door behind me. Time slows down, and the sun comes through the blinds in waves. Waves of sixteen. Waves of June. It's as if I am an older version of myself stepping back in time and righting a wrong.

He lies down in my bed, and I climb up on top of him and start to kiss him. I wonder what his sweet little sixteen-year-old ass tastes like. We get completely naked. A silver necklace dangles around his neck, and my piercings are in my ears, both objects catching flickers of sunlight. My dick is throbbing, my heart pounding. He lies on top of me, rubbing his dick up against me, kissing me. I grab his face and say, "You are so, so fucking cute." He lies on his back so I can blow him, but then I put my hands underneath his legs, glide him to the edge of the bed, and throw his legs up in the air, staring at his asshole, purple and hairless. I start to lick at it while holding his legs up in the air, my hands around his ankles like cuffs or my palms flat against his feet. I lick him while he jerks himself and looks down at me. I love it how he looks down at me. I'm in various states of bliss, pressing my tongue in his ass, his nuts over the bridge of my nose. I can't even touch myself because the slightest touch would make me cum, and I was already dripping it out. The only problem is that he is practically scentless, which, if I weren't so blissed out, would basically send me into a rage. While my tongue is pressed against his asshole, a line of Rimbaud runs through my head: *No one is serious at seventeen*. Let alone sixteen, I think. He looks like Rimbaud, I realize. *Du Bois*, I think.

"Can I fuck you?" I ask him between licks.

"Sure," he says, touching his dick.

We both stand up, and I bend him over my bed. I put a condom on—as if that's necessary—put some lube on my fingers, then spread it over his asshole.

"It's cold," he whines.

"It'll warm up," I lie. I shove my cock inside him, and he's tighter than I ever thought possible. I pump in and out once or twice and hear him make a groaning sound. He says "dude" in a breathless, dreamy sort of way, which turns me on. I looking down at my dick, up inside him. Like a stupid sixteen-year-old, he cums in about ten seconds from jerking himself. We try to keep going, and he lays on my bed again. I stand at the edge of the bed while holding his legs back and shove my dick inside him. I love having sex in total brightness like this. I can see everything—his purple asshole all exposed, wrapped around my cock, clinging to it for dear life. I go in and out deeply, looking back and forth at his asshole and his facial expression, smiling. I fuck his sixteen-year-old ass. I could have done this every day in high school, I think to myself. But then I probably would have fallen in love with him and stayed in town. I wonder what that would be like. Suddenly, I'm sixteen again too, thinking that all I want out of life is to be in love, and it doesn't matter where it happens, but only who it happens with. I pump in and out of him a few more times, his ass spread completely open in the sunlight. It is sublime. It's as if his ass was made to take my cock. But he says to me, "I don't think I can take it anymore, it kind of hurts now," so I stop. I take the condom off and jerk off over his butt. Then we laugh and get dressed.

I want so badly to see him again afterward. I go back to Montreal and write to him, wishing I was in Pennsylvania with him. I send him a mixtape. I act like the complete fool I was back in high school, ever the romantic. I never see him again, so in my head he is permanently sixteen, permanently in my high school bedroom with his legs in the air, waiting for me to give it to him.

*

The rent is cheap, the roommates rather punk. As for me, I think punk but look pretty. I exist on the borders between punk and prince. We live above a massage parlour so there is undeniable proof that happy endings do exist. Just not the kind I imagined. I'm lucky to be living with roommates with whom I have things in common: sexual politics, mainly, but also music, some books. Michael decorates the apartment with stencil cut-outs using electrical tape and spray paint. There is a stencil of Lil' Kim, the Queen Bee. Michael finds a giant number 4 outside, so he takes it, pins it up above the hallway, and spray paints "PLAY" after. 4Play. We dub ourselves the House of Homo Hotties.

The only problem is, I'm the youngest one in the house. I get this bitter vibe from them. I don't know why. My roommates spend a lot of time *talking* about sex, but not very much time actually *having* sex. Me, on the other hand, well, I've been a busy bad boy. One night, I'm at a party called Cruise Control. Mostly androgynous lesbians, so I can't afford to be picky. After downing a few PBRs, I go for a boy named Antoine. A couple of beers later, we're on top of a couch in the middle of the party dancing and kicking around and making out.

The next morning starts with a loud thud as Antoine falls out of my tiny twin-sized bed. Drunk-ass. I notice that my wallet—on the bookshelf next to my bed—is missing twenty dollars. Antoine is still drunk, and doesn't understand me. "Let me see your wallet," I say to him. I check it: nothing.

He smiles at me stupidly, less cute in the daylight. Almost falls over again while he's putting on his skinny jeans. "I think you stole my twenty dollars," I tell him. "Okay, sweetheart, there you go—shoes on. I think it's time for you to go. I have some work to do. Au revoir, dude." He walks by Michael and Alice (the other roommate, a stone-butch lesbian), creating an awkward lull in their pointless, circling conversation about Foucault. I walk past them to the kitchen to make coffee, avoiding eye contact, holding back a smile.

Michael calls out to me, "You're ridiculous."

"I know."

"He was kind of a babe—why kick him out so early?"

"Think he stole twenty bucks from me ..."

"Oh, hey, my name is Arthur. Life is so hard, I got laid again, life is so hard."

"Yeah, yeah," I say. "You two could get laid if you wanted to. It's like I've been telling you—too busy talking about sex to actually have it."

"Ha," he says. "All for the poetry, right?"

"Exactly," I say.

*

I spend most of the winter wrapped up in bedsheets with different boys. The city is wrapped up in a sheet of its own, sleet, snow, and ice. I write a lot of poems, focus on school. Occasionally, someone sticks around for two months at a time, I grow fond of him, his smell, his body, his hows and whys. But then he leaves. We're young so we don't need reasons to leave. We are free to drift as we please. I keep their favourite clothes and wear them like ghosts. I get cold. I need a heavier coat with more feathers. I've been inside of others' bodies, too busy to lift away from my own.

*

you look younger than you are

*

The chat screen blinks over and over again: *1 MESSAGE*. I click on it, and the profile comes up along with the message "allo." The username catches my eye: crazyinthebrain. The profile shows a young guy; there are only a few photos. In one, he's sitting in a school desk wearing a white T-shirt with his elbows on the table, head tilted. He looks like a bad boy in after-school detention. There are also mirror shots, a yearbook photo. I'm intrigued. There is something about him. His name is Jeremy. He looks sad and infinitely hopeful all at once. His hair is an impossible shade of faun. Innocent grey-blue eyes mesmerize me.

*

And to think he was coming over just for sex. By the time I opened the door, his parents had already driven away after dropping him off. His coat was hideous. He had acne, and his hair—the most distinct shade of strawberry blond I'd ever seen—was frozen and sticking straight up in the wind. I took one look at him and thought, *Oh fuck, why am I always so horny?* As we walked up the stairs, I took a deep breath to calm myself. *After all, there is a* dépanneur, *a convenience store, right across the street*, I thought. *At the very worst, I could just drink and get on with it.* It wouldn't be the first time. I still feel guilty for my reaction to him during that first impression. Not that I ever told him, but still.

I took him up to my room. When he took off his coat, I noticed how pale Jeremy's skin was. Little by little, he started to seem more attractive. I considered how the cold tends to make the complexion worse. I realized that his style was the only thing turning me off, not him personally. I looked him in the eyes as we made awkward pre-hookup conversation, noticing how his minor acne looked more like a nerve-induced breakout than an ongoing problem. I could picture his face without the little teenage blemishes and saw that he had lots of potential. Razor-blade sharp cheekbones, goofily cute ears, piercing blue eyes, big lips, everything symmetrical. His hair, however, was spiked straight up. While we were making out, I patted it down and held it there, staring at him, already aware of his muse-like qualities.

He smiled coyly looking down at me. There was something peaceful about him—he smiled so easily. I like to think that I fell in love with him the first time I watched him sleep, which was that very same night, but really, it was probably within those first moments that we were making out. He occasionally looked up while still on top of me and played with my hair, which seemed so affectionate for a first rendezvous. He played and sniffled, not even looking at me, like I was his *thing*. I think he knew it, too. Through the window behind us, it was grey outside and the snow was falling—things were happening. The palms of my hands groped his ass, and my hands fit perfectly. It was plump in a way that young guys' asses rarely are. I told him that he had the most amazing ass I'd ever seen, and he used this information to his advantage for years to come.

"What do you want to do?" I asked him.

"I like to suck cock," he said confidently. "What do you want to do?"

"First, I want to suck you. Then, I want to lick your beautiful ass—and then, I want to fuck you." He smiled bashfully.

Jeremy wore black briefs with a red skull and crossbones design on the side. I peeled them off him, laughing to myself at their ridiculousness. Who would wear something like that? Who was this guy? The suburbs spit out these young, gorgeous guys into the city before they got immersed in ego and image, and they could be stupid-sexy with no effort.

Once I got him fully undressed, I sucked him for a little while, but only to earn what I wanted to do. "Okay," I said. "Bend over the bed." Aside from having the nicest ass I'd ever seen, he also had the cutest, pinkest asshole imaginable—if you took a strawberry and sliced it in half horizontally, that's how pink it was. It was just pornographically pink—impossibly pink and puckered. It perplexed me, his pretty asshole. Anyone can see it now, though, since it's all over the Internet in one of his little jerkoff videos. After rimming him until my tongue was sore, I put a condom on. He was impossibly tight; I can only imagine how it would have felt raw, but I never did that back then. It didn't look like he was enjoying it much, but I put my hand on his dick and it was rock-hard. I looked down at the little dark-blond hairs that followed the direction of my dick as I plunged in and out of him.

"Do you like that?" I asked him with that tone of voice that suggests you don't particularly care about the answer. But with him, I did care.

"It's okay," he replied.

"You're so fucking beautiful, so fucking ..."

"It's better when you say that," he said.

After some thrusting, it was all over. Jeremy was the first boy I ever came inside.

I had no choice but to let him stay the night since he had no way to get home, and for once, I actually didn't mind. We smoked cigarettes and started to have real conversations. This was typical of guys my age: it was always easier for us to actually talk *after* the sex. We dated in reverse, or we didn't date at all.

"So ... you're almost finished with high school, huh?" I asked him.

"Yep, and after that, I move to Montreal for college. I can't wait." His accent, totally Quebecois, was animated and seemed cartoonish to me then—I was a sucker for it. He told me that he wanted to study film, to make movies, to be a director. An artist! What a pleasant surprise. We talked about David Lynch films—great taste for a kid. I was relieved that unlike so many boys I'd met, he had a passion.

"Do you ever go out?" I asked him. I wanted to make sure he actually seemed as sweet and genuine as I thought he was, and wasn't some vapid village vampire.

"I did once, but it's hard being underage. But I like it, you know? I like the gay village. I like how the spirit there is so liberated and free, and people can just be whoever they are, do whatever they want to do, and no one will judge them."

It had been a long time since I had heard anyone say anything positive about the gay village, so his freshly optimistic and honest insight struck me. The gay village was one of Montreal's claims to fame, the biggest one in North America, after all. The gay ghetto. We had an entire stretch of downtown to ourselves—clubs, bars, restos, saunas, massage parlours. The clubs were the dominant factor—there were five or six of them, all around since the early '90s, multilevel megaclubs. The '90s never ended in Montreal. Thanks to the separatists and the French fact, the city had gloriously managed to mostly bypass the cultural homogenization of globalization and gentrification that most cities south of the border went through.

"Yeah, that's true. There is a sense of freedom there," I said. "There's something else about it, too. It has this tendency to bring out the worst in guys. It's like an attitude factory. I think it takes in these perfectly decent young guys, and if they aren't careful, they get swallowed up in that scene. It can be like a black hole. They go in uncorrupted, and overnight turn into these ultra-vain, fashion obsessed, shallow party boys. I don't understand why. I don't think the culture was always like that ..." I say, not entirely sure, trailing off.

I could tell he didn't really understand the kind of person I was talking about. I didn't mind, though—he'd figure it out eventually. He took a drag from his cigarette and said, "The worst kind of people tend to stand out the most, I guess."

We fit together perfectly in my twin-sized bed. He fell asleep with such ease, which was peaceful and reassuring to me. I stayed up, propped over him on my elbow. I looked at Jeremy and then out my window at the light snow falling and the moonlight. Things were happening, but the night was calm and still. I felt an odd realization surge over me—unwelcomed, uninvited—the total perfection of the moment. I watched him fall asleep that night and thought, *Oh fuck, oh fuck, I'm going to fall in love with this guy in the hardest way possible, and he has only had sex with, like, three guys, and we're way too young—he's way too young. Montreal will gobble him up and spit him back out a new person—we're way too young for how this is going to feel.* I had no choice but to embrace it with the totally relentless abandon that comes with intense amounts of bliss.

*

very very bright moments that flicker and fade

*

I tried to lie to myself about it at first. Our second time hanging out, I took him to a party. We went outside to smoke a cigarette together.

"Look," I told him. "I like you a lot, but I don't want a boyfriend. I think monogamy is sort of weird. I want to see you, but I don't think we should limit each other." I was so full of shit. I could tell he looked disappointed. He looked down at the ground and said, "Okay." Even as I was spewing the polyamory party line (I had just read *The Ethical Slut*), I had a sense of detachment and disbelief in what I was saying. I was just going through the motions, using some new philosophy to try to back my way out of being, well, scared. He looked sad. We took a taxi back to my place, and I fucked him again, but this time it was different. The warmth that he radiated with last time just wasn't there.

The next weekend, I called him, but he was busy. I had that gut feeling you get when you know something is wrong. He told me he was with his ex.

I talked to Michael. "I need some advice. If you really liked a guy, but he was only seventeen and finishing high school—but you wanted to be with him—what would you do?"

"What are you getting at?" he asked me. "I mean, what are you *actually* worried about?"

I hesitated. "He's seventeen and I don't want to be judged by my friends for dating a seventeen-year-old," I admitted. Michael looked me in the eyes and said with punk-rock honesty, "Oh, come on. Who fucking cares what other people think about it? Do what you fucking want."

I called Jeremy on the phone.

"I can't really talk right now," he told me.

"Okay, but listen. Um, all that stuff I said before, fuck it. I want to be your boyfriend, like, if you still wanna be."

"I'm very, very happy right now. I'm very happy you said that. But I'm around some people right now so I can't talk. Um, I say yes. Talk to you soon. Bye."

*

"I love you but I don't want to be one of those couples that says 'I love you' to each other all the time," I said. "It's tacky."

Within a week we were one of those couples that said "I love you" all the time. We even invented different ways to say it, different intonations, inflections, softly and loudly. It was the cutest thing you'd ever seen. It was disgusting.

And I loved it.

*

We would Skype all the time, and he would come to see me when he could get a lift into the city. I was in love with a boy that worked at a gas station and was finishing high school. We'd talk about casual things while he ate chips, smiling for what seemed like no reason; he had a natural goofiness that I took a liking to. I had just turned twenty.

The first time that I went to see Jeremy in the suburbs at his parents' house, before he moved to Montreal was just on the eve of summer. I found it bizarre going out there—after all my efforts to move to the city, here I was going into the suburbs. I took the bus. It was so dark that I couldn't see the street signs to know where to get off. I almost missed the stop, and a part of me panicked about getting lost. I couldn't ask for directions because my French, at the time, was still next-to-non-existent. But at one intersection, I saw him.

He was waiting for me in the rain. It was just us, the sprinkling sky, and the streetlights. His hair was still its natural colour then; that spring was the last time I would ever see him with his real strawberry-blond hair. Getting off the bus that night, I realized how exceptionally beautiful I found him (before anyone else did). His hair was wet and flat and not spiked up like a stupid teenager's. I could tell, even back then, that he was about to bloom, but I don't think I was aware of the gorgeous destruction that I would be part of in the wake of that blooming. He had cheekbones that could cut diamonds. Whenever I looked at him, I felt drunk. I didn't tell him all of this right away; I kept it to myself, and I should have kept it to myself much longer, because once someone realizes they are beloved they will torture you with it—a lesson one assumes they will never forget.

We walked back to his house, and the smell of his skin caressed me with every breath I took. I was glad I met him before he got into the city, or before the city got into him. I loved walking with him out there on the deserted streets—it was erotic, but not in an earned and obvious way like in the gay bars. He dressed differently back then, too—an oversized hoodie, jeans that didn't hug his legs. I was caught somewhere between horny and in love. On the walk, all I could think about was fucking him again, but this time in his high school bedroom. People move all the time—if you move, the ghosts of former rooms don't necessarily haunt you. But if you fuck in a room the other person will always remember, they'll always remember you. And before him? I was never remembered, and never remembered anybody.

He lived in a big house with a large backyard and a nice family. There was a piano and framed art on the walls. His family was cultured. His mother was kind, and she seemed to take a liking to me instantly. I wished they were my family, and in time, they started to feel that way. He took me down into his room in the basement. That summer it became our little cave, a world we carved out against and away from the real world. When we were down there, we were either naked or in basketball shorts. Our cave of youth, filled with cuddling, kissing, films, and sex. Down there, time collapsed.

*

During that summer in his room, he kept showing me his important little mementos that he kept inside a box. There was a letter from his mother that she wrote to him when he was younger, long before he came out, which he was instructed not to open until he was older. After he came out, he looked at the letter. In it, his mother said that she would always love him forever, no matter what, no matter how he turned out, straight or gay. The box also contained a condom wrapper from when he lost his virginity (to a girl). And one of the poems I gave him, a sonnet. There was a condom wrapper from when he took my virginity (half of it, anyway—the half that could actually mean something to a guy because it's so much harder to let someone into you than it is to just fuck someone). I picked up the wrapper.

"You still have this?" I asked him.

"Yes, I keep all of them, all the first times," he said.

He had a big dick, and it hurt. I never wanted anyone to do it to me, but there we were in his bedroom, in that basement. I thought to myself, *It's now or never.* I only did it because I wanted him to be the one to do it; otherwise, I thought of myself exclusively as a top. That's how I knew I was in love with him. The first time, it was like a revelation. It felt so incredibly full, and it was strange to feel what I'd been doing to others, an intimate and invasive feeling.

At some point during this time, I started to cry because I realized I was in the bedroom of the guy I loved, and he was opening himself up to me in the way that mattered, showing me things from his childhood, things only I got to see. I realized intuitively how rare this was going to be in life, even more rare than I had imagined. Out of nowhere, I started to cry. I was terrified but also joyful, sublime, hyperventilating, hysterical.

"I'm so sorry. I love you so much, I'm so fucking sorry," I sobbed to him.

Jeremy smiled, almost laughing. He loved my craziness. "What's wrong? Why are you crying?"

"For every moment that I've treated you less well than I should have. Like last week, when I spent the night here but was grouchy to you in the morning. I said you were being lazy and that you were going to be late for school, but I don't care if you're lazy! And later that day, I felt so guilty. When I saw you get off the bus, wearing your bright purple shirt, walking home, toward me, it was like a vision."

Years from now, Jeremy will tell his current boyfriend about that day: how after he got off the bus, I surprised him with a picnic in the backyard—with the help of his mom—to make up for the grouchy morning. He'll say to his boyfriend, *You're going to have a hard time impressing my mom. Shit, I shouldn't have told you that.*

"There are these moments when everything speeds up and slows down at the same time, and suddenly I realize where I am," I said. "Everything is perfect, synched up. I really love you, and it scares me sometimes. When it gets that far out, it's hard to imagine life without it. I'm sorry for any time when I acted like I didn't know this." I was still sobbing, soaked in tears.

"It's okay," he said, softly. "I really love you too. Don't worry."

That night, he mixed orange juice and coke (when coke was just Coca-Cola) together and it tasted surprisingly good. I loved being at his house. We would sneak around while his parents were asleep, as if we were two brothers separated at birth by borders and circumstances who had finally found each other. He would "shh" me whenever I was too loud. There was a devious, cartoonish quality about this midnight snacking. He would look around the corners before continuing—getting caught, after all, would be embarrassing. The light from refrigerators has never looked the same to me since. I watched Jeremy drink orange juice in his underwear, illuminated by the midnight glow. All that vitamin C flowing into his bright white body. He was my teenage sensation.

*

A year and a half later, I tore through his room in Montreal at five in the morning in a post-coitus, gin-soaked fit, trying to find things—the pictures, the ring that "is not a promise ring," the condom wrapper, the fucking poetry I wrote for him (sonnets and villanelles) that he used to put in his high-school binder. I couldn't even find the box, let alone the evidence that he had loved me once. He still had makeup all over his face, the remnants of his drag persona, that evil woman Fantasia, and he kept asking me what I thought I was doing, to stop it, telling me that I looked ridiculous.

*

After fucking, we would smoke a cigarette outside and talk to the spider that had built a web on his front porch. We named him Alfred. "Alfred doesn't speak English," Jeremy decided. "So you're gonna have to learn French."

*

One night we fucked quietly in his backyard while his parents slept, me on top of him, my fingers inside him. I asked him a few weeks ago if he remembered this night, and he said yes. Every star was in the sky that night, before they froze over and fell down like snow and got crushed and sniffed up like piles of blow. I could feel his asshole tighten up just past my knuckles as we came at the same time, a reoccurring event, and for a second I felt like my palm behind his head was itself a crescent moon and he was the earth, his gravity spinning me dizzily around his pretty body.

*

It's the summertime again, and a muscular blond
kisses you as a joke. He is drinking a blue Slush Puppie
and takes a sip of it. You're outside a club.
He asks if you want a taste of it, you say sure.
He kisses you with the slush in his mouth.
It would never really happen, you think.
Four years later, he's on his hands and knees in front of you.

*

I call Jeremy on Skype.

"Allo!" he answers.

"I'm freaking out," I tell him.

"What's the matter?"

"They asked me to move out. We just had another 'house meeting,' and they asked me to move out. Fuck! I can't afford to move! The rent is only $250 a month here. I can't afford something else. They said I wasn't contributing to the 'communal feel' of the house, or something ... I think they're just jealous of me and you, though."

I start to cry on cam.

"It'll be okay," he says. "You'll just find a new place. A better place. Those assholes are obviously totally neurotic, anyway."

I sniffle. "You think so?" The reassurance is extremely comforting. Something is happening in this moment. "I just wanna say thank you ... because, um ... you're the only person I have. I don't have any real friends. I mean, sure, I have friends, but none of them really get me. They're all a bunch of pretentious hipster assholes always trying to out-cool each other. You're the only person who sees who I am. I can't thank you enough for that."

To Jeremy, who's still in high school, I am the cool university student who has it all figured out. He looks up to me. But actually, I'm broke, in between apartments, living in a foreign country.

"You'll be okay," he says again. "It's not that big a deal—you'll find something else."

*

After a two-week-long search for a new apartment, I found an agreeable summer sublet in the Mile End. It was awkward moving out of my old apartment. I'd lived with those people for a year, and I talked to them every day. I thought I was close to them. I never saw them again.

I gradually began to understand that this was life, and this was going to keep happening, over and over again. You can't really trust anyone. You don't really have any friends other than the people whom you *fucking love*. Unless you have wept and shouted with that person, held each other, gone through the void together, they aren't truly your friend, and even then, it still sometimes doesn't work out. I started to accept this.

In my mind, Jeremy was becoming something else to me—not just a boyfriend, but a kind of brother. I knew that no matter what happened as roommates came and went, this relationship wouldn't go away. I took that to heart. It was as if he was a childhood friend and we had found each other again in another life, a better life. That summer, he would come in from the suburbs to stay at my place for two, three days at a time. It started to feel like we were almost living together. I always wanted him to stay all the time. He was only seventeen, but I didn't care. A teenager. He let me fuck him even though it hurt. One time, I fucked him in the shower, and the lube washed off from the hot water. I could see the blood dripping down his leg, but he didn't tell me to stop. I would cum inside him, even with the condom on. The room I lived in felt like our own little studio, set apart by a long hallway from the rest of the apartment. The washer and dryer were in that room, which always gave it a domestic ambiance, calm, with the scent of laundry, the smell of linen in the summer.

One morning, a spider hung down from the ceiling. It must have been Alfred, following us, checking up on us. Jeremy woke me with a nudge. "Spider!" he said, pointing at the ceiling. I looked up to see Alfred hanging there. As if in a dream, in an instant Jeremy's arm collapsed, falling back over me, as he fell right back into dreamland. Alfred retreated to his web. I went back to sleep, my arms locked around Jeremy, protecting him.

It's midway through the summer, and despite how well everything is going, I can't shake the feeling that I still want to fuck other people. I see other guys, and I want to have sex with them. I want to feel limitless. On one hand, I am really in love with Jeremy. On the other, I don't see why our love for each other should necessarily limit us. After all, sex is just sex; it's just pleasure, bodies. If I'm sexually attracted to someone else and have sex with him, that doesn't negate my feelings for Jeremy. It's just a physical thing, a hunger. We can't realistically think that, at this point, we'll be the only people we have sex with for the rest of our lives. It's like how I know in the back of my head that we won't be "together forever," or that we're "too young" to settle down, too young to feel this in love. I want to face reality. Why can't we have the best of both worlds? Why can't we have young love *and* boundless sex? Plus, it's obvious that we're both tops. The sex we have is great, but it's rare that he lets me fuck him anymore, we just have endless foreplay. I figure we can just experiment, and if it doesn't work—we'll go back to being monogamous.

I call him up and tell him all of this, all my justifications and philosophies about it. He is hesitant, but he agrees to it. We're going to be in an "open rela-tionship." Which means we're occasionally allowed to have sex with other people. I don't see what the big deal is. It's unrealistic to do anything else. It's not like we're old and looking to move in together and get married. We can be in love and also express our youthful desires. It won't change anything. *Il faut être absolument moderne.*

Jeremy moves into the city to a college residence at the end of the summer. It is the beginning of the end of us.

PART 2
sleeping with ghosts

Jeremy turned eighteen a few weeks ago, so we've started going out to clubs together. One night, I do ecstasy, a drug Jeremy hasn't tried yet. It has a little imprint of Marilyn Monroe on it. The warehouse we're at is packed, and everyone is sweating, which will probably smell wonderful in about thirty minutes, but I'm concerned about my body temp. There's some kind of cabaret or drag performance happening on stage, and a pair of drunk assholes in front of me yells at one of the girls on stage, "Yeahhh, suck it, bitch!" I'm feeling very happy, but against my will. I say, "Whoa … that's … kind of … sexist," trying to be more politically correct than I really am.

They look at me and back to the performer. I'm rolling hard. One shouts, "Yeahhh, you heard me, I said *suck it*, bitch!" Once the drag queen on stage stops yelling, "Res-ist con-scrip-tion!" in a German accent to the beat of "Good Vibrations," they turn around to take a closer look at me. I start to shoegaze so they won't see my pupils. The guys notice the water bottle in my hand—a dead giveaway—and become interested in me. I look up out of awkward anxiousness—do they have to do this while the endorphin bomb explodes? They smile. I smile too but only because I don't want to be unkind. Empathy overload. They start to chat me up. I try to answer, but the bubblegum I'm chewing makes my mouth water too much, and all I can do is laugh at or with them and quietly grind my teeth.

I look around for Jeremy in drag, but I think he's still getting ready. That's the thing—we always go out together, but we separate as soon as we arrive. Sometimes I wish he was around to help me tell others to fuck off. One of the guys in front asks me something, and I say, "Mmm," and before I know it, these hair dressers, bartenders, raptors, bad dancers start to hug me. I stumble away and, after searching the party, walk up to Fantasia, possibly interrupting a conversation about pop art, though more probably about penis size. We kiss through thick synth.

In character now, Fantasia yells, "What're you doing here? Havin' fun?"

I shake my head, rub my face against her glittery neon breasts. They don't seem fake anymore because everything is so fake that it has become real. I tell her about the predatory raptors/hairdressers.

"Fantasia take cara that," she says with a toothy smile. She rolls out the palm of her hand and snorts some pixie dust, blowing some in my face, rolls out her own personal red carpet, then struts away. I go outside and light a cigarette that I wish would never end. The music from inside is fading in my head, the night sky turns black, and I nod off again.

When I wake up, my arms are wrapped around Jeremy, his makeup washed off, my hair dishevelled, and we are ever so casually hungover, still inspired, cool.

*

Before I met Jeremy, I was fucking this guy named Jon.

"Why don't you like him?" Michael asked me.

"I don't know," I said. "I don't like the face he makes when he cums. Plus, he hides his asshole when he gets fucked, all timid-like. It's weird."

"So you don't like this guy because of his O-face?"

"Yeah, I guess so. And because he hides his asshole. What?" Michael was laughing.

"Then why did you agree to have sex with him as many times as possible in a single week?"

"Because it's summer," I said, like it was totally logical. "And he's only in the city for a week, so ..."

A few days later, Jon was in my room. We were naked and had just finished having sex again. Now we were getting stoned. I hadn't smoked weed in months, and it hit me really hard. I stared at him, astounded.

"You're hot," I told him, as if I was just realizing it for the first time. He was really skinny, looked like an elf.

I didn't understand how we did it, nineteen-year-old or early-twenties guys; we managed to look perpetually sixteen. He was talking and I wasn't listening. I kept grabbing my dick, distracted. I was so tired of having sex with him, but I didn't want to talk to him either, so all we could do was fuck. I was glad he was from the States and didn't live here. He was obviously falling in love with me, and it was getting annoying.

*

Winter is beautiful, I don't care what anyone says. Why does everyone bitch about winter? The walk between the Crémazie Metro station and the residence where Jeremy lives is long and cold as fuck, but walking there becomes a sort of meditation. I go to the front of the building with its big glass doors, and I can see him in the hallway wearing silver-grey basketball shorts. His hair is grown out long and dyed blond now.

I see him after class most days of the week, and we spent the whole winter like that, in his tiny residence room. It's a space that would normally make someone feel claustrophobic, but for us it's a sanctuary. It gets dark outside at three p.m., which means we are basically always in the dark, surrounded by our own brightness. We stay up late showing each other random music and art. We suck each other off, he sits on my face, I eat his ass and worship him. Sex between us is just something that happens in the blink of an eye now, a form of play. We spend so much time in bed together that Jeremy has invented a term for it: com-codda, which is what "come cuddle" sounds like when you say it really fast in a Quebec accent. Com-codda becomes a state of mind, a make-believe place that exists only between us, in that bed, underneath that sheet. It was a Temporary Autonomous Zone. We have entire days and nights played out in minutes in com-codda. Underneath the covers, we pretend that we just woke up, roll over to go to work, and come back. It is our world and no one else's.

The only downside to all of this beauty is that both Jeremy and I are entirely broke as fuck. I am good at being broke, but Jeremy isn't used to it. He isn't used to losing weight from not eating as much as when he lived at home with his parents. I take a poetic pride in the struggle, even though my poetry professor says, "There is nothing sexy about poverty." We manage to get by even though, a lot of evenings, our dinner choices are basically bread or instant white rice with salad dressing on it, something that Jeremy insists tastes good. Or, to switch things up, we crush Ramen noodles inside the bag and eat them raw. I am too busy eating ass to notice how hungry I am.

Jeremy is so broke that winter that one month he can't afford both food and rent, though he works twenty hours a week at a *dépanneur* in addition to going to college. He is nearly failing his classes because he's working so much, and probably has undiagnosed ADD. As the first of the month creeps closer, he sits me down.

"I did something for money without telling you," he says.

"Oh boy. What was it?"

He turns on his computer screen and goes to a website. "I did a porn video!"

I look at the images, crisp and radiant. I'm not sure how I'm supposed to feel—upset? Isn't this something people normally get upset over? Instead, I'm curious.

"Well, let me see it!" I say.

First, he reads me the video description: "Blond twink boy Chris Laurent is a college student and aspiring artist of sorts. Although he's fairly new to the gay world, having only come out within the past two years, he is remarkably open-minded and relaxed about it, possessing a confident demeanour well beyond his eighteen years. Chris is in a relationship, but the rules are far from 'traditional.' He lets us in on a personal story of how he used a game of 'truth or dare' to get what he wanted."

They do a little interview with him, asking him about the first time he had sex. That's the truth or dare bit. He tells them that he was ten and dared another kid to let him suck his cock. They ask Jeremy about his relationship, and he says he's in one, but it's open—"We're experimental, so doing porn is okay." He says that he likes guys with dark hair who are a little bit older yet still boyish—that'd be me. Then the real stuff starts. They show him lying on a blue couch jerking off. Then he turns around on the couch, showing off his ass, arching his back, reaching back with his hands and spreading his cheeks apart for the whole Internet to see his gorgeous pink little cherry. I get hard from watching it. I have to admit, it's really well done.

"Wow," I say. "I can't believe you did that. But I guess it's not bad. How much did they give you for it?"

"Three hundred dollars!" he says, happily. "Now I can pay my rent!"

"Yeah. So ... do you think you're going to do it again?"

"I don't know, maybe. Does it bother you?"

I hesitate for a moment. "No, I guess not. I mean, it's just porn, right? I don't see how it could affect your future. They'd just be solos, right? People are going to recognize you, though. You realize that?"

"Yeah, well, whatever. Who cares? It's not that big a deal."

*

waiting for
the evening
when you
will again
in winter
kiss me
naked in
your living
room & tell
me kid-grinning,
after I just drank
vanille française coffee,
that I taste
like pancakes

*

Jeremy is, well, I don't know where, actually. He has stopped replying to all of my texts. On purpose, probably. He's been acting distant lately, just replying whenever he feels like it.

This boy named Phil comes over. I just met him on the Internet. He's eighteen and really short. He sits on my bed. I haven't fucked someone besides Jeremy since I tried to fuck some guy in his thirties but couldn't get turned on because he only had one ball. And a toothpick dick. Phil looks like an angel, and it freaks me out. Phil reads philosophy. Nietzsche confuses Jeremy. I tell Phil to chew some gum before I kiss him, but he doesn't have any. I go to the washroom to get the toothpaste and come back. I smile at him, squeeze toothpaste onto my finger, then shove it into his mouth. He laughs, the white paste drooling out of his perfect mouth. He spits. I start to kiss him. I lick the back of his neck slowly, all the way down his back, and start going at his ass. A moment of sheer panic consumes me: does he have a nicer ass than my boyfriend? That would be a major blow to us. I calm down, fumbling around for a condom, packages of free lubricant from parties, lubing up his asshole, my cock, rubbing the rest on my bed without a care. I put my arm around his neck while I'm fucking him, biting his ear, smelling his hair. He just lies there on his stomach, which is hot to me. I think of the first time I fucked Jeremy. I think of Phil. Everything goes bright white and I can't believe it but, "I'm going to cum, I'm going to cum inside of you, okay?"

"What? Yeah, okay."

I have not come inside a guy since Jeremy, and I know why—a guy has to be stupid-sexy for that to happen, assuming you're wearing a rubber. Or maybe he's just really tight.

*

"Would it bother you if I started turning tricks?" Jeremy asks.

Yes. "No. It shouldn't. I don't know. Do what you have to do."

For hours at a time each week, Jeremy runs off with Michel. I block it out. Michel looks like a troll that you'd find underneath a bridge. He's well into his sixties and says things to Jeremy like, "Oh Jeremy, you're such a nice boy, such a sweet boy." Jeremy makes fifty dollars every time he sees Michel, every time Michel sucks his dick.

Jeremy expands his client list.

"There are other ways of making money," I suggest. I don't want to admit it's getting to me—we're supposed to be radically free, liberated.

"But I am so fucking sick of being poor. I'm so sick of not being able to have anything nice. Why does everyone else get to have nice stuff but not us?" It's a very good point.

"I don't know, monkey. We're rich in other ways. It'll all pay off eventually."

"It's bullshit. It's that capitalism stuff you talk about."

"Break it all apart, insist on full collapse," I mumble.

"Felix has a ton of nice bags, and all of those twinks down in the village have everything paid for. What about us? We're going to work in call centres forever!" he says, practically screaming. The mere thought of this sends me spiralling toward an anxiety attack. He continues. "There aren't any goddamn jobs! My parents won't give me any money!" I try to console him, hugging him.

"I'll be able to find a good job once I graduate and learn French," I tell him, trying to convince myself. "It'll all be okay."

*

"Why have you been such a little brat to me lately? Every other word is 'shh' or 'shaddup.' You're only nice when you're in the mood for affection and you drain me because you know I'm an infinite resource. Are you trying to get me to love you so hard I stop loving myself?"

"Prada. Prada, Prada, Prada. Gucci? GaGa?! Prada. Prada Prada Prada."

"Probably? It really hurts when you say things like that. I treat you like a prince and you know it. You were never like this at first. I'm not a doormat, you know. If you keep this up, I'll fucking leave you. I can fuck anyone I want. Would you even care?"

"Armani, Gucci. Fendi. Fendi Fendi Armani."

"I know the whole polyamory thing was my idea, but I did not say I was okay with how you're using it. It's supposed to just be physical. We're supposed to just fuck other guys, what the fuck? But you text other people. I won't even give Phil my cell phone number. Sex is physical, but texting? Texting is emotional. I mean, you're not supposed to go out alone purposely to hook up with other guys, it's just supposed to be like if it happens, but you're using it as a way to keep me from going out to parties with you so that you can go out alone with your fashionista fifs. Fashion is counter-revolutionary. And you guys do bad drugs. Coke is so passé, Jeremy. Up the ass, not up the nose. Come on."

"Prada ... Gabana! Dolce, Gabana! Prada Prada!"

"Babe, look. I know you've been upset ever since Alexander McQueen died, but seriously, you just found out about him, like, two months ago. There's plenty of other McQueen's in this McWorld. Get over it."

"PRADA!?"

"And another thing, I never agreed to you having a sugar daddy. It's like all you talk about now is fashion."

"Valentino ..."

"Don't try to sweet-talk me. You fucked up Valentine's Day, remember? I bought candy from Jean Coutu and all you gave me was a mediocre blowjob. No card. What do you mean Jean who? Jean Coutu, fuck. The store, dude. What did we even do? Hang out and watch *The L Word*? You take me for granted. I know you're happy about all the clothes you can afford because of your new sugar daddy, but seriously, Jeremy."

He ignores me. "*Teeth*" by Lady Gaga comes on in the background.

"He has to take out his dentures to suck you! That's so fucked up I can't even breathe when I think about it. I called the police on an older man once, and I'll do it again. Dentures?"

"... Prada Prada. Coco!" He snaps his fingers.

"That was one fucking time, okay? We were wearing sailor suits, it was roleplay, I was drunk! Whatever. At least he had teeth."

*

I am a victim of Halloween. I don't know where he is, and it's my fault. He's so fucking stupid—why do I love him? Why do I put up with all of this just for the electric-blond heroin high he gives me? Liked him better when he was a chestnut. Was my idea to go blond. Once he went blond, he never went back. Blondness is brutal. Makes me bitter.

Text from his friend Felix: Jeremy is not with me. He lost his phone. If he's smart, he'll know where to go.

I reply: What kind of friend are you? It's almost November and he's in a Go-Go Boy costume. That means he's wearing only underwear and he has no wallet or phone and he's downtown. Go find him!

Felix: Non. Ur annoying. Shut up.

Totally evil little amateur porn star. I am drunk, crying, and I call my mom, but there's no answer. I consider calling his mom, the police. Someone will rape him. He'll get beat up. Some creep will put GHB in his drink. Should have gone as Gizmo like I said, but he had to go GoGo. After midnight he is a Gremlin. Oh my god, GHB. It is three in the morning but I am spazzing out, so I take a bus down to the village to find him. He is standing outside the club in a fur coat.

"You're downtown at three a.m. without a cell phone or a wallet in your underwear ... smoking a cigarette."

"I know. I look great."

"Yeah. Yeah, you do, and I totally want to fuck you right now, but your stupidity is consuming me. What would you do if I didn't come down here?"

"The same thing I am going to do now that you're here. Go to the apartment where Felix is."

We walk inside and Britney Spears is playing. Everyone stares at me talking with Jeremy.

"*As-tu dansé avec les beau mecs?*" they ask him right in front of me, not realizing that I understand. Like he doesn't have a *beau mec* right beside him. But this is the world of excess: one is never enough. They are the epitome of village trash: straightened hair, high-pitched voices, bleeding noses, choking Trojans, your friendly neighbourhood ghetto-homo-HoMa retards working at Couche-Tards. None of them are in college; they can hardly pay rent, but they have designer purses paid for by men with dentures. Twink trash for cash tricking at Taboo. Jeremy changes his clothes, and we take the bus back to his residence, hardly talking. Try to sneak past the security guard, get caught, con him with our good looks like we always do. If you're young and beautiful, you can get away with anything. Even slowly breaking the person you love apart without him doing anything about it, just like you said he wouldn't.

*

One of the things I've always loved about Jeremy is that he gets my sadness. He's never once judged me if I go off the deep end a little bit. He gets my obsessiveness, my drive. He gets the ups and downs, the total abandon, and he'll pretend to be a wolf and howl with me in wolf-voice at the top of our lungs—"*I Looooooooove Youuuuuu!*"

Still, since I came back from Christmas break, I can't shake this horrible feeling. I feel fucking wrecked, so guilty I can't eat. I can feel something missing: the magic. He doesn't admire me the way he used to, and I recognize it. I want to get out before he gets out, but I can't bring myself to do it. Phil keeps telling me to do it. It's been like a mantra in my head, a sick voice that screams at me whenever I look at Jeremy, and I feel like I'm going insane. The voice says, *I'm not attracted to you anymore, I'm not attracted to you anymore, I'm not in love with you anymore, I want to break up with you, You make my stomach feel like it's dropped through the floor.*

I'm sitting on his bed. It's pitch-black outside, as usual. We're in our lovely little shoebox of a dorm room. I lean back against the wall. I start to hyperventilate. It makes a sound that comes from my gut. I start to sob uncontrollably, snot dripping from my nose. *I—hohh-uh, hohh-uh, hohh-uh,* I try to breathe but can only make weird noises. I can't speak.

"What the fuck?" he says, caught off guard. "What is it? What's the matter?" His voice kills me. I can't say what I want to say to a voice like that, a voice I love so much.

I continue to gasp for air. I make horrible noises like I've been punched in the stomach. He rubs my back, tells me to breathe. Finally I can muster up sentences. "I love you and there is something on my mind and I'm not saying I am thinking about anything but I am thinking about what it would be like to think about it and it makes me feel so extremely guilty and sad, infinitely sad. I walk by houses and think about what it would be like someday to live in a house with you and how nice that would be. Then I think about how that will never happen. Fuck. Why can't we have something like that? I think about how this has to end. Logically it will end, and then I think about if I should end it, and I'm not saying I want to end it but that I think about thinking about ending it. I don't want to break up with you. I don't know what it is. There is this thought loop in my head I can't get rid of, and it's making me feel crazy. It tells me I should break up with you because I think you want to break up with me and that I can tell you're thinking about it too, or that you've thought about it, so then I think about it." I am crying like a little boy during the entire speech.

He looks straight into my eyes and says in an indignant tone, surprised, "Are you thinking of breaking up with me!?" and the shock of his voice renders me helpless, and I burst out, "No, I don't want to!" and I try to explain to him that I think about it because I think about him thinking about it.

He pauses, considering this. "I have thought about it," he admits. "But I don't want to. I love you. We're great together."

I sniffle. "We are? We are ..."

I hug him and pivot my head into his chest, breathing in the smell of him, relieved. Winter dreamland continues.

*

On our one-year anniversary, Jeremy and I go with his family to the Quebec countryside to stay in a chalet for the weekend. I've never done something like this before. It's great to be with his family—his mom, stepdad, little sister, grandma and grandpa, everyone together. But something—I can't tell what—is bothering Jeremy the whole time we're there. His mother takes some photos of us standing together outside in front of a lake, but he just looks annoyed. Around the cabin there is a bunch of folkish Quebec memorabilia, things Jeremy remembers from his childhood but I've never heard of. He shows them to me, playing old folk songs, laughing to the lyrics, but I just stare blankly since I still don't understand the language, even though I started to learn it this winter. Something dawns on me; I see how much he relishes this old folky Quebec stuff.

"You really love Quebec, don't you?" I say to him.

"Yeah, I guess?"

"I mean, you'll probably never be able to leave it," I say, looking down, realizing this for the first time. He'll never be able to move to the United States with me; he'll never be able to leave his home.

During the entire trip we can't have sex because we're in such close proximity to his family. We're doing something really official and "serious" like this, so I figure things must, in some way, be okay. Yet he goes on four-wheeling trips with his sister and leaves me alone for hours without saying anything about it.

At night we lie together in a big sleeping bag and watch a movie on his laptop. I try to bring it up and he tells me to "Just shut the fuck up, drop it." In the morning, we take a shower together. The sun comes in through the window and mixes with the mist. Jeremy washes my hair from behind me while casually stroking my cock. My eyes are shut tight to keep out the shampoo and the sunlight. I'm smiling and laughing, but something seems wrong. I can feel it in his touch, the sensuality and the slowness of his hands as he washes my hair, that something is very wrong. *No, I'm just paranoid.* But I can feel it. He's thinking, "This is over," but he isn't sure how to end it, how to cast me off so that he can grow alone.

*

"Why do you treat me so badly?" I ask him in the dorm room.

He ponders the question. "Because I know that I can treat you however I want and that you won't do anything about it," he says.

"That's really horrible of you to say."

"I know," he admits. "Sometimes when I go out alone or with Felix and I ignore you, it's because I want to know what it feels like to be single. I imagine what it would be like to not know you. To be free. But then, I come back and I see you, and I think to myself, *What the fuck am I doing? Why do I wonder what it's like to be with other people when I have this great, amazing guy who loves me so much, who I love too?*"

*

"You are looking extremely thin and it is worrying me," says your poetry professor.

*

I'm hanging out with Phil in my bedroom. I tell him that I should probably break up with Jeremy but that I won't because I love him too much.

"But he treats you like shit," Phil reminds me. "Why would you stay with him?"

"Well, because I love him."

"That is really stupid. You're an idiot. You should break up with him and be my boyfriend," he says, like it's all so simple, and maybe it is, but I don't know. I explain that I can't break up with Jeremy because as much as he hurts me, it would hurt me more to hurt him.

"You guys aren't even in a real relationship anyways," Phil says dismissively. "This open relationship stuff. You basically already cheated on him with me."

"Open relationships aren't bullshit—"

"Yes, they fucking are."

"You just don't understand the logic behind it. It's unrealistic to expect people at our age to be committed to each other."

"No, it's not," he says. "Why do you always say stuff like that?"

"It's not like we can just settle down and stop living."

"No, you just don't *want* to. But don't say it's not possible. You're choosing to be like that—typical urban gay stuff. I know people from high school who were together in high school, and they are still together. It happens," he says. "It's a choice."

"But that's totally ridiculous. They're completely lacking in experience. It's kind of sad."

Phil laughs, looking at me incredulously. "It's not *sad*, you pretentious Plateau asshole, it's *normal*. They love each other, they only want each other. There is nothing sad or tragic about it. In fact, if you and Jeremy were as in love as you claim to be, you'd be more like them."

*

I make the long, cold walk from Crémazie Metro station to Jeremy's residence. When I get there, he's sitting on the couch watching TV. I sit down and try to cuddle up next to him but get no response. It suddenly dawns on me that all our pet names are gone. The admiration is gone. The person beside me is a different person. I stand up in front of him, cross my arms.

"Do you still love me?" I ask him.

"Yes!"

"Okay. Do you still want to *be* with me?"

The question lingers in the air for a few seconds too long before the sharp and sudden pain sets in. I nod. Jeremy puts his face into the palms of his hands.

"I knew it." I lean against the wall, and the tears come.

He starts to cry, and I can't tell if it's forced or sincere. We both realize that we will not always know each other even if we want to. As much as we love each other, it isn't enough because adulthood will fuck us up. This is just the beginning of our lives and not the end and, no matter how hard we try, we're not forever. I'm shocked at how hard he ends up crying, looking confused and guilty, because he almost never cries.

"I wanted to tell you earlier," he says. "I've been trying to think of a good time to do it. I still love you, though, so it doesn't make any fucking sense," he says.

"Then *don't*," I say.

"No," he says. "We have to. We're too young to be like this. I feel suffocated. I need to explore, and not just sexually. I need to be single. And so do you."

"But we're in love," I remind him. "We're in love, and we're supposed to be artists together, move to New York together, be unstoppable. What the fuck happened to all of that?"

"I can't. I'm not ready for that. This is too much. But I still love you, and I'll always love you." We sit on his bed, hugging each other, crying. I leave, knowing I'll never see that place again. I walk back to the Metro and ride the entire Orange Line sobbing, disoriented, a lost American kid in Montreal.

*

haven't I seen you in a porno
haven't I seen you in the Metro
I think I've seen you on the Internet
I think I saw you and your ex-boyfriend fucking on the Internet

*

I'm walking around the club with my friend Max. He's only a few years older than me but says he is getting too old to come here. It's summer again and the place is totally packed. I don't recognize anyone; I haven't been out in a while. While walking through a dark corridor, I make eye contact with Jeremy, and at first glance, I hardly recognize him. He's wearing tons of makeup, eyeliner, tight black pants maybe made from leather, a mesh shirt ripped strategically, and a black top hat. Very '80s New Wave. Since the breakup, we have a routine when we run into each other at clubs: we make eye contact, I hardly recognize him and do a double-take; he smiles as soon as I see him, and I check out whatever outrageous attire he's wearing. Tonight is no different. After he shows me his outfit, we go our separate ways. I go to the bar and down a shot of whiskey for good measure.

I see him on the dance floor, so Max and I walk up to him. The music is blaring and horrible, as usual. Jeremy looks at me and mimics holding a cigarette. I nod and we head up to the terrace. I've been waiting for this moment for weeks. I light his cigarette, and Max stands there awkwardly until the thickening silence between us signals that he should leave.

I stare at Jeremy. We're eye-level because he's wearing high heels.

"Why aren't you ready to be friends yet?" I ask him. "Is it because you're afraid you won't be able to change or grow if you're with me?"

He looks at the ground. He won't look me in the eye when we get into this conversation, which is telling. "No, it's not that. Clearly I'm changing a lot, if I'm with you or not," he says, referring, I think, to his aesthetic.

"I don't really get why we broke it off. I know you feel like you have to be single, and we had all these problems, but—"

"I know, I know—we wouldn't have had all of those problems if I didn't feel like I needed to be single."

"Right."

I concentrate on smoking my cigarette so that he doesn't notice that my hands are shaking. I need him to agree to be friends. I miss him so much that I feel like I'm going through withdrawal. We agreed we'd wait until after the summer before attempting any sort of friendship. It's not working.

"I can't wait," I say. "I miss you, and I know you miss me too. This feels really unnatural."

"Yeah, I do miss you," he says. "But what would we do together? It'd be awkward. It's too soon."

"If you didn't still have emotions for this whole thing, then you'd be fine with it. You're not over me, are you?"

He hesitates. "No, maybe not all the way."

"Do you still love me?"

"Look, this poster has RuPaul on it!" he says, grabbing a flyer.

"I'm serious. Answer me."

"I don't know."

"Come back to me awhile," I sing.

"Oh God, no. Stop it. You're drunk! You can't sing. *Arrêt*," he says, laughing.

"Change your style again ... come back to me awhile,"

"You're being loud! People are looking at us!" he says, putting his head down, embarrassed.

"Change your taste in ... men."

In an instant, his mood lightens. "Do you like my eyeshadow and lipstick?" He closes his eyes to show off the makeup, sticking out his lips.

"Yes," I say, leaning in to kiss him quickly. "You know, I've been thinking ... If someone told me I had to forfeit all of my memories in Montreal before I met you, before I fell in love, I would do it, though it would be hard."

"It's just that I was with you before I even moved here," he says. "I need to experience other things."

"What do you think that does to me? What are you going to do after you realize how much better you had it? Go and fuck a hundred guys, it's fine. Have other relationships. But don't act like it has anything to do with things between us. What're you going to do when you realize it doesn't compare?"

"I don't know. Deal with it, I guess." Translation: *You'll come back to me.*

I see Phil across the terrace. He throws a knowing glance at both of us.

"That guy is kinda weird," Jeremy says. "He doesn't have a nicer ass than me, huh?"

I've never been asked such a difficult question in my entire life.

"No." I say. "So, this summer?"

"You know we'd start having sex again."

"I know. That's okay. I miss sucking your dick. And I know you miss it with me too, admit it."

"Hush," he says.

"No, seriously, admit it."

He laughs, shaking his head at me. "Yes, okay, I miss it."

I smile at him, shivering in the cool summer night.

"Oh, you look so cold." Jeremy rubs his hand on my arm, my back, trying to warm me up. "Let's go inside."

*

"I had a dream that you and I went camping. We were alone in the woods together. We built a campfire." Phil tells me this a few days after I write a poem about how one of the things he smells like is a campfire. He smells like wood smoke.

But he doesn't know I thought that, never knows about the poem. Maybe Phil and I are delayed holograms of our future selves. A message in a dream. He is a sign of all the possible options, like Jeremy with his *Mr. Nobody* tattoo.

*

The summer winds down and fall approaches. Jeremy and I hook up a few times, and all the love is still there, but then it's days or a week before we interact again.

He texts me to tell me his phone number has changed, which I take as a sign of him still reaching out, still giving me access. Still, he's seeing other people, rebounding with some younger guy. I decide to try to do the same, while always thinking of him.

*

Phil and I try again without realizing we're doing anything at all. Every time I try to love Phil, he won't let me, and every time he tries to love me, I won't let him. But right now, we're drinking gin and tonics with lime in my apartment, and I'm noticing how much he changes when he gets drunk. He goes from being a reserved, guarded boy to my best friend.

We stumble to the Metro in the first blizzard of the season, laughing, senseless. His face is lit up like a kid's on Christmas day. His blue eyes catch glimmers from the colourful lights lining the outside of Metro Mont-Royal. The train comes up and he punches me in the arm, wrestles with me, a form of foreplay. On the night bus home, after the party, his buzz has worn off and he's back to pretending nothing is going on between us. He tries to convince me to wait in line with him for typical four-a.m. food, and I say no. I tell him to meet me back at my apartment, and he gives me this look like, *Man, I can't believe you, after everything we've been through on this night of winter adventure, you're gonna leave me here all alone*, making me think maybe it actually does matter, so I go up to him from behind and hug him, wrap my arms around him, and I see the corner of his smile, a smirk.

"Oh. So you *do* care that I'm with you right now, eh, kid?" I say.

We stand there, swaying slightly. I tower over him, biting the collar on his shirt, pulling it back with my teeth, nudging my face in, smelling the sweat on his neck. After marching through the snow back to my apartment, we collapse into bed. I lay there cuddling him, smelling the side of his face, whispering stupid things in his ear. Lucidly drunk. Haven't really had him in a while, I realize. I tell him how beautiful he is, that I want to fuck him, that I need to be inside his body. We are both in our boxers.

I get on top of him, my knees on the outside of his. I rub his back and hope for the best. I hang my head down as if I'm bowing, kneeling at his pristine, brink-of-passed-out presence. I get on my elbows, shove my face against his ass, smell him through the cotton of his boxers, a thin layer that separates us. I'm fooling around, trying to make him more than half-awake. I peel his boxers off slowly, spread his ass cheeks apart with my hands, and brush my thumb against the hair on his asshole delicately, as if I'm brushing hair out of his eyes. I want to dive in with my tongue. I want to press my tongue so far deep inside his asshole that I could French kiss him from behind. He shakes his little butt in the air, though, and says the words I hate to hear: "No, not tonight, in the morning."

But in the morning, the sun comes up, displaying our confusion in broad daylight—in the morning people are sober, or worse, hungover. I fucking hate the morning. In the morning, a boy wants to take a shower. In the morning, he has to get out of bed to take a piss, and nothing will ever be the same again. The creases in the bed sheets are different. The night before, the beer on your breath still smells kind of sexy and is mixed with the scent of sleep. In the morning, it is just putrid and dehydrated. With Philip I am infinitely waiting for the morning. But nothing ever happens in the morning.

So I lie there on my back, wishing I could just crawl on top of him and pin his hands down, glide my dick up inside his ass without a condom, poke around inside him while he drunkenly drools on my pillows, stare at his beautiful face and kiss him right below his eyebrow on his cheekbone while I shovel in and out of him, digging into his dirt, divine. I lie there in frustration, my finger still tickling his asshole, which is all sweaty and gooey, the natural lubrication of his ass glands. All that masculine musk. I lie there on my back in the moonlight while he is semi-awake, pressing my middle finger into his ass only slightly, like a fuck-you to his insides for not letting me fuck him for real. I pull my hand away and up to my face, high off the smell of his boy butt, and start to stroke my cock while little flickers of his pheromones flood up into my frontal cortex, choking my senses, triggering something primal and adolescent in me, and I'm paralyzed, taken away by his smell, otherworldly; I knew he was an angel or a ghost, and while the smell of the most intimate part of him—his essence—smashes into the neurons in my brain, I cum like an earthquake has struck, as if Quebec has literally shaken and separated off into the Atlantic. When it's over and my hand is covered in cum, he lies there sleeping, and I feel completely distant, separated from him. He takes pleasure in my getting pleasure from him. He does nothing, and afterward I want more of him, while he has everything of me.

In the morning, I'll make him coffee. He'll struggle in English, and I'll struggle in French. He'll leave awkwardly.

*

We romp the bed and all the sheets slide bad
I trick my treats and all is sweet again
I slut I fuck you up inside our lust

The trains go zooming out in blue and white
And boys in bloom glide in
We ride the tracks while all the ice sleets bad

Electro thumps our heads too much
And jumps me out tonight bright black
I handcuff, fuck you up inside our lust

I lube my stroke and all the dudes glide glad
I trick my treats and all is kink S/M
I stub my smoke and the skin sizzles sad

I shift your shaft the way you said
But I lose myself in roles we play
We hop in bed and all the sheets drift jazz

At last when fuck stops it all comes back again
A ruin my sheets and all the boys bloom bad
I slut I fuck you up inside our lust

*

Jeremy drops out of college. I had seen this coming.

"Why are you giving up on your dreams?" I say.

"Shut the fuck up! Easy for you to say. Your parents give you money for stuff. I just don't want to be a fucking director anymore, okay? I wanna be the *fucking star.*"

"But you are a star, babe. I mean, almost all of my poems are about you."

"Arthur, how many times do I have to tell you that no one gives a fuck about poetry? Zero fucks. I wanna be fabulous. I still have time to figure it out. I'll get my second chance," he says with such conviction that my heart breaks a bit more.

"There's no such thing as second chances in this world," I tell him. He doesn't listen.

*

Phil tries to get me to fall in love with him. He comes over to let me fuck him, but he does the most frustrating thing; he won't look me in the eyes. While I pump in and out of him, he looks to the side, giggling and laughing and saying "Ah," stroking himself while I hold his legs up in the air and plunge my dick into him relentlessly. He keeps looking at the ceiling, so I slap him hard on the side of his precious face to make him look at me and acknowledge me. It's me fucking you, Phil, not someone else. This is what you came here for, isn't it? It's my dick with this goddamn, stupid pointless condom on it, my dick pumping up inside you, your asshole all exposed, your legs in the air, all vulnerable. It's my dick and no one else's. This is something you will remember forever, Philip, and when I fucking cum inside of you—and if you don't look me in the eyes, I will. I'll slip the condom off and cum in you. My DNA will be up inside your intestines, a part of you. When I am pounding your coy little boyish ass with my hands against the bottoms of your feet, remember this, Philip: I am holding you up by pinning you down, and in this moment you are mine.

*

I will not come to your apartment and break
your dishes, spit in your face, and tell you
about the merits of anarchism. I will not sink
so low as to make this poem about sex, I will
not get undressed again. I will not even eat
drugs and show up at your favourite club just
to get a hug or get my greedy palms on that bubble
butt again, and then again, I will not even begin
to fathom you dancing with him, hands on his hips,
his annoying lisp. I will not imagine you kissing him
and your tongue sliding in between the gap in his two
front teeth, will not imagine your dick sliding in between
the crack of his ass, will not wonder what it means that
he's seventeen and I will not send another SMS that says
it's not my fault you couldn't handle me. I will run into you
at Berri-UQAM in total calmness when you pretend we
don't know each other anymore, and I hope the Metro doors
shut as soon as you come walking up, pulling me ever away.

*

Phil asks me if I, like, want to hang out, which I think means, do you want to come over and fuck me and spend the night? So I say yes. It turns out that it means something entirely different—these goddamn language barriers are getting old. It's been one week since the last time I saw Phil, when I made the very stupid decision to tell him to sleep on the couch. Note to my future self: you never, ever, *ever* tell a cute boy to sleep on the couch, no matter how gutted your heart is.

I take the Metro to the bus station and then a bus to the suburbs to see Phil, just as I used to do when I was seeing Jeremy. As the city passes behind me, all I can see is the expanse of land and road, carrying me outward. Of course, it is lightly raining again. It's like a clichéd movie scene; it has to start lightly raining again, just as it did back then. I begin to hyperventilate, feeling an immense and heavy guilt for actually liking someone else, thinking how everything people say to each other is amendable, temporary, replaceable—we can say all of these meaningful things when we're in love and then love other people when it's over. Phil meets me at the agreed-upon *dépanneur*, and we walk back to his place, a big, beautiful house. We go down into his bedroom. Another cute boy living in the basement of a house in the suburbs of Montreal.

"Why did you come so late?" Phil asks.

"Why not?"

"The bus back to the city won't run again tonight, so I guess you'll have to spend the night ..."

"I sort of thought that was the plan."

"No, not exactly," he says. "You can't blame this one on language. 'Hang out' doesn't mean 'sleep over,' Arthur."

"To be fair, that's usually what people mean when they ask to hang out with me."

We lounge on his bed and watch a movie. It feels nice just to be next to someone. Halfway through the film, I start to feel really sick. I hold up my hand to see if I'm shaking and sure enough, I am. Phil looks upset.

"You need to fucking eat," he says, like he's run out of patience. "You need *calories*. You need protein, you need fat. You can't just make yourself disappear, okay?" He storms off.

"Where are you going?" I ask.

"Come with me."

In the kitchen he calms down, starts to whistle as he makes me a milkshake, then pasta. He looks accomplished, like he just fixed something. After eating, I stop shaking.

Back in bed, Phil starts to sing, "You are my sunshine, my only sunshine" like a blues singer. I'm an emotional wreck, and anything makes me cry these days.

"Please stop singing that," I ask him.

"Why?"

"Because it's sad, and sad things make me think of Jeremy. Please stop."

He looks annoyed. "I'm not going to stop singing something just because it reminds you of him."

Phil cuddles with a cat while we're in bed. I tell him that I'm allergic to cats, though I'm not, because I want Phil to give me his attention and affection. It dawns on me that I am jealous of a cat. The cat doesn't move. Would Phil rather cuddle with that fucking cat than with me? What an asshole. Jeremy would never do something like that. I ask Phil to make the cat leave, but he refuses. So I roll over, expecting that he'll cuddle up next to me, but he doesn't. Holding back tears, I lie next to someone I could have loved. He feels no pity for me, and why should he after all those times he wanted me and probably rolled over in this very bed alone while I was cuddling Jeremy or waiting for him to get back from a night out?

Phil wakes me up in the morning and tells me to get dressed. We walk to the bus station in silence, but Phil and I are often silent, so I can't tell if that's necessarily a bad thing. There is a vast space in his eyes, like something is missing. It's unnerving but gorgeous. I start to imagine him floating rather than walking. I can smell his hoodie from two feet away—it's intoxicating.

"Well, later," he says.

"Okay, bye."

I'm not sure if I'll ever see him again. I'm upset that he made me go all the way to Longueil and then left me sexless.

*

Jeremy has made new friends, best friends, friends forever, because in this moment, they are high on speed and everything feels ridiculously infinite and within their reach. Jeremy is high on speed, drenched in sweat that I wish I could drink. He is high on ecstasy, rolling on MDMA in a club where everyone has had sex with each other. He's dancing next to me. His lines are, *I really do love you* and *Some day I will realize it and be mature enough to handle it,* but he's not saying his lines, he's just dancing, going through the motions that kill the emotions. Jeremy does bumps of coke throughout the night from a little vial that hangs off his necklace.

He is cool. He stays up for three days, tweaked out on methamphetamine and social acceptance. Six months pass by in the blink of an eye, and none of these people are around him anymore. The same goes for me. People move through us like water, and when it's over we're each other's only constant. .

*

Your clothes are still on my floor.
Sweaters, sleeves, briefs you'd leave,
skin you shed, before you left. No more

spending the day in the shirt you wore.
I would wrap myself up in you, to keep
you close for hours, still on my floor.

Needles can't stitch fix this kind of torn.
Gums bleed. On my brush I taste your teeth.
Like skin shed before you left. No more

of my clothes at yours. Shut up in drawers.
The ghost of my body, once in bedsheets—
yours. Cold, hours still on my floor,

needy, naked from the sheets you tore.
No monsters under my bed, I sigh relief:
just skin shed before you left. No more

scooch, spoon, that soft sound, a snore,
no jokes down here about me: pillow thief.
You're closed. I'm still on my floor
next to skin shed before you left. Before.

*

It's November, the beginning of six months of winter, six months of night. I love the smell of the snow, the diamonds on the ground, the crisp frost that hurts my skin in a soothing way. I've become hardened. If you don't let anyone in, they can't do any damage.

Except if you let the old ones back in.

I'm at Parking on Amherst Street. People are smoking in the stairwell; the stench is dark and dank. Jeremy passes by. My heart spits up into my throat, then tumbles back down and pulsates in that breaking way. The nervousness goes from my chest to my arms to the palms of my hands, an insatiable worry—is he okay? Has something horrible happened to him yet? Does he have a disease yet, is he dangerously poor, is he dying, and can I maybe be the one to save him? *I think I dreamt you up inside my head.*

He stops and smiles at me, the same tooth-goofy grin I fell for two years ago. I want to grab him by the ears and make him my Montreal slut. "Hey!" he says. "How're you doing?"

"I'm okay," I confess. "How are things with you and ... Raphael?" I don't really want to know. Raphael is his "new boyfriend" after the first rebound. He's bald, in his thirties, short, but Jeremy saw *something* in him. We argue over whether or not he is balding or just has a butch shaved head. They practically live together, with a dog and everything.

"They're good," he tells me. Life is simple when you're kind of stupid. I decide to cut to the chase.

"He's too old for you, it won't last. I don't know what you see in that guy, Jay. Daddy issues, obviously. So, does he fuck you? Does he fuck you raw, Jeremy-boy?" The idea of someone else getting to fuck him has always bothered me.

There are lights above us, burning hot red lines. These conversations are always more meaningful, half-drunk in weird lighting. Other guys drift past us, whispering about us, trying to hear snippets of our conversation—our story.

"Oh, you didn't hear ..." he starts.

"Hear what?"

"Raphael is positive."

My heart sinks into my gut and stays there. All I can think about is Jeremy getting it too. Close to a minute of silence passes.

"You're eighteen," is all I can manage to say.

"So what?" Jeremy says. Those two words can say so much. So what.

I take a swig of my beer. Blond, like the boys I like.

"You're eighteen, Jeremy, and he's thirty-four, and he has HIV ..." I say, stammering, trying to come to a point.

"It's really not that bad. Really. I promise, we're completely safe. We use protection every time. He's undetectable."

"Undetectable?"

"Yeah, dummy, it means he has a low viral load."

"So ... you broke up with me so that you could end up dating someone more than ten years older than you who is HIV positive?"

"You know it's not like that," he says.

"I swear to god, Jeremy, if he infects you ..."

"He won't infect me."

I look at him, bite my lip.

"Anyways, it doesn't matter. He doesn't fuck me, I fuck him. I do suck him, though, and that makes me nervous. And I have to be careful that I don't use his toothbrush or razors or anything like that ..." he says, trailing off. His voice goes up and down like it always does, like a song. It's hard to stay mad.

*

Jeremy and I don't talk for two months after that, but then I get a text message: I'm breaking up with him. Can I come over? I think, *This is my chance.* He comes over, having just quit a telemarketing job and broken up with Raphael. I think to myself, *Finally. He's going to come back around, my little boomerang. On again, off again, my tourniquet, mannequin.*

We lie on my bed together, staring at the ceiling fan above us, the light strings making a clink, clink, clink. I look at him. "Well, I guess it's okay if we do this now," I say, and I kiss his electric lips. His armpits smell the same. His skin is covered with tiny beads of brilliant sweat. I crush my body into his, his legs on my shoulders, smashing into him, hard. No penetration, just this. I turn him over and worship his ass, licking him, kissing his asshole. "I missed you," I say.

After it's all over, we smoke a cigarette, sitting on the edge of the bed.

"That's exactly what I've been missing," he admits.

"What is?" I know, but I want to hear him say it out loud.

"That ... passion. With Raphael, it was just sex, normal sex. With you, it's passion. I can see you lose yourself."

"It's always going to be like that," I assure him, and myself. "We're always going to have that. That's why I've always loved you so much."

*

Jeremy and I are just friends now, and that's okay, I guess. I'm not going crazy over him anymore. Or at least I'm learning to manage it, to hide it better. We're close friends, but we still have sex sometimes. In those moments, I try not to be so passionate, but I think he secretly likes it. Otherwise, why does he always come back? Anything feels possible now, and I've started to go out more.

I'm wearing a blue button-down dress shirt that looks a bit preppier than what I'm normally into because I'm trying something new. I want to look clean-cut but with a punk mindset. I want to feel everything and be an artist and a rebel and still be, I don't know, happy. It's dark and snowy outside, and that makes everyone feel horny. Blankets cover the city. People cover their bodies with other bodies, anybody's body.

I open up *gay411.com*, that life-changing website where, every once in a while, someone really good looking comes into your life and changes everything. The message box pops up: delete, delete, delete. I'm picky, but that's part of having good taste. Then I see one in the middle of my screen that stays there. Tacoma. Odd username for a gay profile. Tacoma ... Washington. Tacoma is also a kind of truck, I think. Tacoma sounds butch. Tacoma is six-foot-three and his age isn't listed. He has messaged me before, one night when I was drunk, but I deleted it.

The photo, a selfie, shows him shirtless (good pectorals, a swimmer's build), the camera angled down at him, showing half of his face, his blue eyes, the sly, sexual fuck-me-I'll-fuck-you-boy smirk. The background, his apartment, shows real furniture, good lighting, no mess, just order, control. He looks like Phil if Phil were grown up. I wonder how old he is. Since I'm not feeling as dismissive in my sober state, I reply to his "hey" with a seductive yet reserved "hi."

We go on MSN and start to chat. I ask him what he does.

"Construction," he says. That's a turn-on right away. I ask him his age.

"Twenty-four." He asks for mine.

"Twenty-one," I tell him.

We go on webcam so that we can each see what the other really looks like. I worry about my hair. He sees me and says, "good looking." Once I see him, I'm sold right away. He has big arms and wears a simple mysterious white T-shirt. The cam freezes, and he goes offline. I briefly panic—rejection! But then he comes back online. We chat about the typical things.

"Are you masc or femme?" I ask him.

"Masculine," he replies.

"What are you looking for?"

"Friends and sex," he says, not realizing the inherent contradiction.

"But not a relationship?" I ask, wondering, longing.

"No," he says.

"Why not?"

"My choice," he says, which doesn't really answer the question. Something like "too fucked-up for love" would, but "my choice" sounds a lot better.

"Come over," he commands, and so I do.

You can tell a lot about someone from the neighbourhood they live in. That he lives in the gay village gives me some hesitation. Is he going to be annoying, immature? I get dressed and take the bus to the Metro station and then walk from there, getting lost in the snowy streets before finding the right direction. I arrive at the door to his apartment building and am surprised at how close it is to the main strip with all the nightclubs. I wonder how it is that I've never seen him out before.

Walking up the stairs with two beers in hand, I'm slightly nervous. When he opens the door, I see that he's fucking gorgeous, and then I'm suddenly really goddamn nervous. He's still wearing a white T-shirt and, I notice, no socks. As soon as I enter the apartment I am utterly *floored* by his scent. This doesn't happen often—I wish it did—it's the best feeling. I'm like a dog; I can tell right away if I like a guy by his scent. The entire place reeks of his skin or sweat, his essence. He's got blondish hair, so the scent seems high-pitched, like a mixture of lime and lemon, like lemonade mixed with sex mixed with light beer and butt hole. It smells like it sparkles, like sugar. Like the inside of the armpit of someone who eats only fruit. It's a smell I wish I could taste. The most amazing thing is that it's him with his clothes on standing in his apartment, not even naked, it's just everywhere. It's everywhere in his apartment like god or sex.

We sit down on his couch and make casual conversation. His name is Fred, and his email is fredex80, like FedEx. *Fred Express*, I think, *sex delivery*. I'm nervous as hell and drink my beer really fast because he's really good-looking and older than me, and he's probably got his shit together, got his whole damn life figured out, and I'm just a guest in it. His answers to questions are cordial yet direct and concise. I feel horny as fuck. He's so big, broad-shouldered. I ask him how he's managed to have such a nice place at his age. He says he started his own business.

Fred complains that he's often sore from construction work. I ask him if he wants a massage, and he says yes, so we go to his bedroom. It's amazing, but kind of cheesy too—he actually has mood lighting. He lies down on his great big bed, flat on his stomach. I've had two beers so I feel more brave. I crawl on top of this man who is laid flat like the earth beneath me, my knees at his sides, and I start to massage him. I'm still amazed by his scent. I kiss his neck which makes his ass wiggle. We start to make out, and then he's on top of me, which doesn't happen very often. I want him to cover me like a flag, to drape himself over me. His hands are rough, and his English is kind of bad, kind of rustic. Everything about him is filled with sex.

I move back on top of him and lick him all the way down, starting from his neck. I spazz out over his scent—lemons, limes, and ass. I lick my way down to his asshole, and there it is—that's the smell. He has one of the most amazing-smelling asses I've ever encountered. But in the flashes of his mood lights, I notice a problem. His asshole protrudes. It's fleshy and sticks out, looks irritated. Since he's a top, it should be delectably tight and untouched. I am immediately turned off. I don't know what to do, and waves of confusion and panic wash over me. But the smell, the intoxicating lemony-ness of his asshole overtakes me again, though I wonder if he has anal warts. Or is that just what an asshole looks like after years and years of anal sex? Or maybe he's a sex-addict, and this is the fifth time today that he's going to get fucked. Or maybe he's into fisting. All the possibilities! I throw caution to the wind and stick my tongue in it anyway. It is soft and fleshy like a sponge. It grosses me out, but I am enthralled by his scent. I want to get his Fredness all over my fucking face. I start to hump my dick against him, and he keeps trying to slide my raw cock into his asshole. I'm so tempted, but the weirdness of his hole is keeping me in check.

"Do you have a condom?" I ask him.

"No, I don't think so."

"Fuck. You have to have condoms somewhere."

After what seems like disappointed hesitation, he digs around and finds a condom. I put it on my dick, shove my dick inside him, and start pounding him hard, not holding anything back. He is on all fours, taking it like a champ.

"You like that, huh?" I ask him. "You like it when skinny, young twink boys fuck you up the ass, don't you?" I say, spanking his hot jock ass. But his asshole is so loose that I can't really feel anything with the condom on. Still, I'm just happy to be inside this man; for once, not a boy but a man. Never done this before. And I'm fucking him hard too. He might be taller, bigger, older, stronger than me, but it doesn't matter. "Take it, you little doggy bitch boy," I tell him.

Afterward, we lie there for a little while, talking about nothing, bedroom talk. I feel strangely comfortable with him. It's bizarre—I topped him, yet I want him to cuddle me. Fred doesn't seem into that. I watch the snow fall outside on the beautiful dark street. I want to stay there in his apartment, safe forever.

"That was really hot," is all I can think of to say.

"Yes, it was very good," he confirms. "A-plus."

*

In a dream, Fred has built a very big house, but he won't let you in, and you cry, begging him to let you in. Instead, he locks you out and won't say why. You did something wrong; it's your fault for being a dramatic, stupid boy. It would have been a good house, but you had to go and fuck it up. As usual.

*

A few days go by, and Fred finally texts me. I take comfort in the momentary confidence that the feeling of distance was all in my head. I go over to his place to spend the night.

After I finish fucking him—literally as soon as we are finished—he turns the light off and rolls over. What the fuck? I have found out that he's actually thirty-one. Shouldn't he be ecstatic that twenty-one-year-olds are still interested in him? He just needs to soften up. I can't stand people who act like they are the only ones who've ever been hurt. It's no reason to deny your own vulnerability and shut off. I put my arms around him and kiss the back of his neck over and over again, burying my face into his spine, nudging the middle of my forehead and the bridge of my nose against the dip in his upper back, between his shoulder blades. It's amazing how two bodies can fit together. I kiss and kiss. He just lies there like a goddamn bag of bones.

"Do you want to cuddle?" I kiss him.

"You can just keep doing that," he says.

"Hmph!" I unwrap my arms and roll over to the other side of the bed, away from him. "You just want to take and take, dude," I tell him.

He rolls over and spoons me hard. In a coy voice he says, "Oh, is that what you want, huh, kid? You want some affection, poor boy?" His big forearm is around my chest. I place my hand over it.

"Well, yeah ..." He holds me like that for a good five minutes, which feels more meaningful than it should.

*

lying in the dark next to this beautiful man you ask him
do you believe in god?
sometimes, he says
you ask him—do you believe in love?
seconds pass
non, he replies
pas non plus

*

He has a really big black truck. We drive around in it. "The Passenger" by Iggy Pop plays in my head while we cruise through the city. He drops me off at Saint-Laurent and Mont-Royal after a quickie. The smell of his ass is all over my face again. I wear it like cologne. We're holding up traffic behind us.

"Bye," he says.

I look at him, waiting.

"I don't kiss goodbye," he says. I can't tell if he's joking or not. I look at him like, *Are you fucking serious?* He laughs and leans over and quickly kisses me on the lips. I get out of the truck and walk into the night.

*

It's Thursday night. I go out because Fred isn't texting me to come over. I figure he's probably just busy, no big deal. I run into Jeremy, who's at the club with his annoying friend. I say "Hi" and then blurt out, "I met someone. I'm really excited about him." Without even thinking about discretion or pacing, I pull out my phone and show Jeremy a picture of Fred.

Jeremy's annoying friend says, "Oh ..." I look at him, and he says excitedly, "I fucked that guy last night!"

My stomach turns. "Was that the first time you guys hooked up?"

"No, second time."

"So what do you think of him?" I ask, wanting to strangle the kid. And also myself, for being such a naïve idiot.

"I don't really know. We just fucked. I was high on ecstasy, it was four a.m. A grindr thing, hon."

"Did you wear a condom?"

"Uh, no."

"Ugh. What do you know about him? I mean, did you guys even talk?"

"I know that he's, like, all heartbroken over his ex, so he only wants sex from people. Why are you so curious?"

"I really like him," I admit. "Do you?"

"No. You can have him."

The next day I wait and wait, hoping that the kid hasn't said anything about our talk, but then I get a text from Fred: "Good job on running your mouth. Hope you're happy."

*

I apologize and tell Fred that I won't talk about him with my friends anymore and that I can't help it if he fucks people that I know—and that I know a lot of guys my age. It feels weird to apologize for something that isn't my fault. But I bite my tongue. He gives me another chance.

In the morning, he tries to fuck me raw, and I want him to, I really want him to, but I say no because I know he fucks other guys raw. And because I need to be emotionally connected to want to get fucked.

"You're right," he says. "We shouldn't do that, it's a bad idea." Does using condoms when we have sex mean that he cares about me more? When he does it raw with other people, does it mean he's closer to them? Or does it mean he respects them less? It's hard to tell what that thin strip of latex really represents—if it brings us closer together or separates us by protecting us.

*

I'm having breakfast with Fred. Well, he gives me some coffee while he gets ready for work and eats toast. Close enough for me to think that we are dating rather than merely fucking. I'm totally delusional but don't realize it yet. We have completely inane conversations that I think are really deep and loaded with subtext. I also continuously try to remind him of my accolades and accomplishments, in some vain hope that he'll want a poet as a boyfriend.

I sip my coffee. He chews his toast with a bored expression on his face.

"So ... how's construction going," I say.

"It's fine. But I work too much."

"Totally want to fuck you in your work boots."

"C'est possible," he says.

"How much do you work, anyway?"

"Fifty, sometimes sixty hours per week."

There is an awkward pause while I consider how much time that is, realize how often I see him, and then understand that work is a way bigger part of his life than boys. I try to come up with something to say to make myself sound busy too.

"Well, I graduate college soon. Then I guess I'll start working too. Not sure in what, though. Writing doesn't exactly pay, but I'm starting to get some poems published, and I was shortlisted for a prize and almost won $500."

"Good job," he offers flatly.

I keep trying. "I wonder what it's like to be older, like you," I say. "You know—to have some money, a nice place, to be stable."

He laughs. "Probably not like you think it is, kiddo. And I don't have that much money. Do you want more coffee?" he asks, then "No?" before I can actually answer. I take that as my cue to leave.

It's cold and sunny outside, which puts me in a good mood. I put on my coat, then my book bag. He opens the door for me to leave. I try to kiss him on the lips but fail. The kiss somehow turns into a double kiss-kiss on the cheeks. I just have to be patient. Soon he'll ask me to move in with him. It's winter, and I can offer endless warmth. It's impossible for someone to block off their emotions forever.

*

I think about the time I ran into a friend at a warehouse party that I'd gone to without Jeremy when he was still my boyfriend. The friend asked me how it's going with Jeremy.

"It's intense."

"What do you mean?"

"I love him so much that it fucking scares me."

He looked at me like I was crazy. Like it's crazy to be so in love that it scares you. Like there isn't anything scary about loving someone that much.

*

—it could have been with anyone! At anytime! In any dumb city! Nothing is fated. Everything is random, the argument continues—

*

I've brought Fred a bottle of wine for his birthday (he's turned thirty-two) and tell him I have to ask him a question.

"I just wanna know if, like, we're just fucking, if it's just sex, or if there's something more," I say.

He smiles bashfully. "No, it's not just sex," he says reassuringly. "But it's not anything serious, either."

"Okay, but do you think, maybe in the future, it could be?"

"Maybe some time in the future," he says. "A long time from now."

If I could have read between the lines, I would have left right then, but I took this comment as better than nothing. We drop the subject. He tells me that he'll save the wine for us, for a special occasion.

A day later, I get a text from him: *j'espère que tu as le bon temps avec moi, mais c'est trop. On se revoir dans une autre vie.* I stay up all night wondering what *autre vie*—"another life"—might have been like.

I never see Fred again.

*

I must find another Fred—that is the only solution. Replace him. I'm at Unity, getting drunk. I see a guy who randomly kissed me in the stairwell a few weeks ago after handing me a drink. I walk up to him. He doesn't remember me, or at least he pretends not to. He lets me hang around him all night, buying me drinks. He's French, mid-thirties or so, he says, but really handsome, a stud. He puts his hand down my pants, grabbing me. We leave the club together and venture back to his BMW, which is parked beneath a condo. These rich dudes and their tacky cars and tasteless condos. The harsh fluorescent lights in the parking garage don't do him any favours. I see the tiredness, the lines on his face.

We get into his BMW, and I bask in the new-car smell. He unbuckles my jeans, reaches over, grabs the back of my head, and forces me down. His dick smells incredible. I suck on it and try to take the whole thing. I lap up the smell of his pubic hair. I'm not used to this; he doesn't smell or taste sweet like a twink, but has a more manly, musky scent.

"Good boy," he says. I unbuckle my jeans too and start jerking off while sucking him. He has one hand on my head, slightly gripping my hair, and the other he slides down my back, down to my ass. He fingers my asshole, then licks his finger to get it wet, then goes back at it, shoving one, then two fingers inside of me while I choke on him.

"Fuck," I mutter, gagging over his cock. If there were room in the car, I would have taken him. I get brave and lift up his ball sack while sucking him and tickle my finger over his manly asshole, but he doesn't really let me.

The whole time, I'm thinking of his husband ("open relationship") sleeping above us in their condo while he fucks some twenty-one-year-old kid in his car. I don't feel bad about it. I think, *Maybe they're open and they will let me be their third. Their houseboy, muse. It could be cool.*

As I'm about to cum, he tells me to "be fucking careful" and looks pissed off when I accidentally get cum on the leather. After it's over, he buckles up his jeans, and all I can think about is the full feeling of his fingers inside me and how I want to still feel full like that. I want him to bend me over the hood of the car, pin me down, and fuck me till he unloads in me. I ask him if we could maybe do this again sometime, and he gives me the lines. I love the lines; they're always so inventive. Everyone has their lines, their lies. His are: He's going away on business to Paris next week and won't be back for two to three weeks. He thinks this is probably enough time to make me forget about him.

"Okay," I say. "That's fine. But I don't have any money to get home."

He throws about thirty dollars at me, practically emptying his pockets. He laughs when he does this, trying to make me feel like a little hustler. I should have asked for more.

*

Jeremy, ever the good, loving friend, gets me through the breakup that is not even a breakup because Fred and I weren't really together. All of the feelings I have for Fred go right back to Jeremy.

I'm so drunk on gin that I'll probably need to go to the hospital in the morning. I take a cab back to the east end with Felix. He knows what I'm trying to do, and he supports me. Jeremy is back at the club dressed to the nines in drag, staying after hours with scene queens and rich daddies, trying to make something happen. I stuck around as long as I could.

"This is so nice of you to let me come back with you," I tell Felix. "Uh, Jeremy didn't exactly tell me to meet him back at his place."

"Whateva, whateva, *j'men fou*," Felix says. "Jeremy is so stupid. He's *lost* without you, anyway, so it's probably for the best if he gets back with you. I mean, that's the only reason he dumped you—to lose himself then find himself. Don't worry about him, *bébé*. Of course he still wants you." Felix says all of this while touching my leg suggestively. I shrug and lean my head against the window, listening to the sound of the snow crunch as the cab rolls along slowly. The east end is my favourite part of town, the underdog neighbourhood. Unlike the trendy Anglo-centric Mile End, out here is where I find authentic Montreal spirit, the right mix of bohemian sensibility with trash and working-class grit. It's barely gentrified. Figures that I first ventured out here to fuck that boy I lost my virginity to.

The cab pulls up to Felix and Jeremy's apartment. Dizzy drunk, I climb up the spiral staircase to heaven. Once inside, I lie down on Jeremy's bed. No matter how many times he moves, it always manages to smell the same, like his high school bedroom back in the suburbs.

"*Bonne nuit*, crazy poet boy," Felix calls out from the next room.

"*Bonne nuit*," I say, face down in a pillow full of feathers.

*

I black out and wake up some time later to blurrily see Fantasia standing in the doorway, carelessly throwing her high heels across the room, makeup smudged, lighting a cigarette with one hand while the other presses against the wall, which she dramatically leans against.

"Hi ... babe," I say timidly.

"I *knew* you would be here, Arthur. You're becoming so predictable."

"I'm very ... reliable," I say. "Please don't kick me out, I'm so drunk."

"I'm not going to kick you out."

"Good! Considering how you were flirting with me all night. You *wanted* me to come back here, slut."

Fantasia throws off her black wig, revealing wild, faded blond hair underneath. Now he's just Jeremy again, with a bunch of eye makeup on. He crawls into bed with me and I attach instantly, happily, in a big spoon. The kissing starts. We roll around on the bedsheets, and I imagine layers of makeup fading off him as he goes back to who he used to be, way back when.

"I missed you," I say.

"This doesn't mean anything," he says with his finger over my lips.

*

In the morning, my hangover is so bad it feels like an icicle has been lodged into my brain. Jeremy forces me to drink water, and it won't stay down, which is mildly terrifying. I'm in severe pain and yet so happy that I spent the night with him, happy that I'm fucked up so that he has a reason to take care of me now. I'm between various states of shivers and sweats as he feeds me freezepops in a fevered mess. Pedialyte. *Du reste pour un péd*é. I lay in his bed for hours, partially because I can't move, but mostly because there is no place else I'd rather be.

*

Now that we've been broken up for a long time and we're just "best friends," "chosen family," "brothers," and other nearly meaningless temporary terminologies that mask our youthful confusion, Jeremy can do whatever he wants, and my input is merely suggestion. I can't help but feel like this is all somehow my fault.

"It makes perfect sense," he says.

"Oh, you tranny hooker," I say, exhausted. "This is so weird. Why don't you just turn tricks *as a guy* like everyone else? Do you get off on doing it while dressed up like a woman?"

"No! See, you don't get it! That's the entire brilliance of it," he says, smiling his bright, beautiful smile. "If I do it like this, no one will know who I am. I can put an ad in the paper, go to the massage parlour, go around the city, and no one will recognize me. I have total anonymity. If I do it as a boy, people will recognize me."

"That's true, I guess."

"Besides," he says. "I'm a pretty lady."

"A pretty, pretty lady," I confirm.

*

It's 3:30 in the morning, and besides fingering this cute sixteen-year-old boy's asshole while I pin him against the wall, I've had no luck at the club, so I bike over to where Jeremy, presently Fantasia, is working. It's a surprise visit. I drunkenly bike from Saint-Catherine up to Ontario, cruising along the street, sniffing and sucking on my finger, past Fred's apartment, looking to see if the lights are on inside, muttering *fuck you, fucking dream dasher asshole* as I bike by. Biking around Montreal at night after a party is pure poetry. I pass streets with names like Rue de

La Visitation and Rue Saint-Timothée. Cruising along Rue Ontario, I see various sex workers, including one named Naomi who, a few months ago as a boy, pinned me to a bathroom stall, shoved his tongue down my throat, tried to force coke up my nose, and then begged to blow me. She looks better as a woman, more natural. It's a nice bike ride. For once, I don't see cops harassing sex workers and other late night revellers. Every couple of blocks, signs flicker in the windows offering four-hand massages. The architecture looks particularly pretty in the golden dim of the streetlights, paint old and faded, cheap-looking yet gorgeous in a classic way. I pull up to the parlour and park my bike outside, locking it. A black curtain hangs in the window with a neon light inside that reads Trans Zen. I'm briefly reminded of another neon sign I saw on a church: *La Salaire De Ton Péché C'est L'enfer. Le Paradis n'existe que pour les justes.* Whatever.

I ring the buzzer.

"*Bonjourrr, Trans Zen, cheri ... comment puis-je aider?*"

"*Allo. Je suis un ami de ...* Fantasia," I reply.

Inside, I am escorted to the lounge area. Fantasia is there smoking a cigarette, her legs crossed, looking trashy high femme.

"Hey! What're you doing here?" she asks.

"I left the club but didn't feel like going home. I wanted to stop by and say hi."

"This is Alexis," Fantasia says, introducing me to her friend. Tall, thin, straight black hair, sexy.

"Alexis, this is Arthur, my ex. He's in love with me. Ha ha."

"Hello, cutie," she says to me, then turns to Fantasia. "What were you think-ing, breaking up with this one?"

"You'd have to get to know him first, dahling," Fantasia says.

Alexis smiles at me. "Touch my boobs." She grabs my hand, laying my palm flat against her breast.

"Well, they're nice," I say.

"That's it!? Just nice!? Do you have any idea how much these things cost?" she says, throwing my palm away.

"Oh god, sorry. I forgot they were fake."

"Spider!" I hear Fantasia yell from across the room, stomping around in high heels. Even dressed as a woman, I can still see the remnants of a goofy teenage boy.

*

Completely heartbroken and hollow over I'm not even sure who anymore, I go to a party to meet a boy from France named Matthieu. I'm pleasantly surprised at how cute he is in person, with wavy black hair, big brown eyes, a slender soccer-player build. We spend the night drinking and talking about the lightest of subjects, things that aren't even real to me, but he's sweet and nice so it works—for now. I go back with him to his apartment and spend the night, and he's an impeccable cuddler. His apartment is furnished and homey; clearly this is not a boy lacking funds. We're both hammered, and I just don't care anymore, really, so I fuck him raw, an incredible feeling. My refusal to do this before has ruined multiple relationships. He feels amazing; his small frame the perfect fit and his insides warm against me.

We spend most of the winter like this. We go for breakfast in the morning: ten dollars for toast, eggs, fruit, sausage. It's sunny outside, and the newspapers are in French, which I can now read, the waitress is nice, and the old men smile at us. We would make a really adorable couple. Matthieu wears a cute scarf, and we talk about the future, about living in France versus living in Canada or the United States. I impress him. He shows photos of me to his friends back home. We eat breakfast but have little to talk about. When it's freezing outside, no one cares. The sex is good, the food is good. *Just get me through the impending snowstorm.* I have a real job now, copywriting, and some money, and I can even call in sick to work if I want to, just to spend the day in bed, warm and cuddling with Matthieu.

Even Jeremy tells me, "That boy is sweet. Just be with him," but Jeremy doesn't understand the feeling that I get when I ride around in a taxi with him, compared to riding around in a taxi with Matthieu. Or how, when we cook dinner together, Matthieu and I have almost nothing to talk about, but when I cook dinner with Jeremy, it doesn't matter if we have nothing to talk about. Jeremy is alone during all of this and not even remotely jealous, but the significance of this does not register with me. Everything is temporary, and only one person really matters.

Wrapped in bed sheets, you have to wonder if the person next to you is much more than a pillow. Are you more than a body wrapped in bed sheets to them, something to keep them warm at night, a human teddy bear, or are you something real, something of consequence, significance, and permanence?

*

I'm lying in bed with Matthieu. We've been seeing each other casually for a little over two months. I don't have serious feelings for him, but I love how affectionate he is—he gives affection so freely that he reminds me of myself when I'm not hurt. But finally he has had enough of my usurping of his affections. I'd been worried this might happen, but I understand. I'm not going to lie to him and give him false hope just because I like the sex or I like the warmth of his body next to mine. I know when these things need to stop, before they get all fucked up, and it stops like this:

He is spooning me in bed, and the lights are off. I sleep soundly with him; the affection is calming, reassuring, not passionate. Matthieu says, "I love the way you smell." I try to think about what he means because I understand the power of smell. I ask him if he means cologne or something else, because if he means something else, then he's hooked on me, it's chemical.

"No," Matthieu says. "I love the smell of *you*, your smell. It drives me crazy." That word—crazy. I love that; it's been so long since someone told me that. I hesitate for a moment and then return the compliment, telling him that I like the way he smells too. I say it too slowly, too awkwardly, a bit too late. He calls me out on my bullshit.

"No, you don't. You can't smell me the way I can smell you. I know it. It's okay." He keeps his arms around me. I apologize. "Come to think of it, I'm always the one cuddling you," he says. "I cuddle you so hard, Arthur, and you don't do anything about it. I give you so much love. And you, well, you just want to take and take." He doesn't say this sadly; he's just stating the facts, that the exchange is uneven and that this is a problem. I could be that asshole and could tell him *why* I don't have big feelings for him, or I could lie and say maybe I will eventually. But there's no need for any of that. I tell him that he's right. We fall asleep. Over the next two weeks, we casually fall out of touch like nothing happened. I see him at a nightclub later on, and I avoid him. I feel bad, but I don't know why. He lets me feel it by doing nothing.

It takes me months, but eventually I miss him, his nearly unconditional affection, his quiet love. And then I remember it, once it is gone long enough—the way he smells.

I tell him this. He tells me to take care.

*

Jeremy and I go to get tattoos together. As the needle drags on our skin like a record-player needle on vinyl, I realize that this is the opposite of music. When music hits the air, it's gone. You can never capture it again. But when ink hits your skin, it's there for life. You'll remember forever the person you did this with. You're tethered together.

*

It's a hot, humid summer day in Montreal, and we're not too poor anymore. It's the type of day where all the flowers seem to be blooming at once, and the spiral staircases look like archetypes of the human genome.

Jeremy and I have passed into a loving kind of friendship—I don't know what it is, exactly, but I like it. We're lying on Felix's couch playing with a puppy. Jeremy's legs, his thighs, still so porcelain white, sprawl out over mine. We're both wearing mesh basketball shorts. In these moments, I never want to leave this city. I feel like I'm with people I will know for decades, a thought both unfathomable and desirable. Part of me says *never leave*, and I want to get *chez nous* tattooed across my knuckles. Another part of me is getting bored, wondering what's next, knowing that no matter what, I'll always be an American ex-pat here. It will never make sense to stay unless I have someone to stay for, unless I'm in love. Real love. Reciprocal love.

*

Once a month or so, I'll be at a party where I'll meet someone strikingly beautiful and think, *This is it, this is the next big thing,* and then maybe we fuck or maybe we don't, but either way nothing happens, so it's back to Jeremy's bedroom, high on Adderall, casual sex, spending the night, smoking weed and eating ass, pretending it's all part of a normal friendship ...

*

Our summer a cycle
of psilocybin
& waves
upon waves
of hot mistakes

*

Jeremy and I have been hooking up quite a bit lately, and I'm getting addicted to it again. He can tell, I know he can tell, and he likes it that I'm addicted to him, to his boy cherry. I bike over to his place after another party and stumble up the spiral staircase to heaven yet again, knock on his door, and he answers, but he isn't having any of it.

"I'm not in the mood," he says. And then he adds, "In fact, we should stop doing this."

"But babe, you were in the mood three days ago. What's with the sudden change of heart?"

"I just don't feel like it anymore."

"Oh, now that you know you have me in your pocket again, it's not fun for you anymore, eh?"

"It's not like that," he lies.

"Then what the fuck is it?"

"*You're old news!*" he yells, pushing me out, slamming the door.

I stumble back against the guard rail, infuriated. I've been pulled in and pushed out so many times I can't keep track. In a fury, I punch the glass panel on the door, accidentally putting my hand through the glass, shattering it. Tiny glass shards fall like diamonds, like snow.

I pull my hand out of the hole that I made in the glass panel and stare at the shards in my hand, watch the blood ooze out of the gashes. It's my left hand, too—my writing hand. Plus, I just broke the law in a foreign country.

Felix comes storming out of the apartment and onto the balcony and screams at me: "*Câlice de tabarnak es tu rendu fou, est-ce que t'es complètement folle toi, tabarnak!* Leave, go away, you're fucking insane, get out of here! Jeremy, get him out of here, *câlice.*"

"Fuck, I didn't mean to. I thought the glass was thicker," I say. The numbness of the alcohol is wearing off and the pain setting in.

Jeremy comes out and looks at my hand, taking it into his. I knew I'd find some way for him to hold my hand tonight. He takes me into the bathroom without saying a word. I start to sob and plead for forgiveness. He says "shh" and "we'll talk about it tomorrow" with impeccable calmness.

"You hate me, don't you?" I ask him. "I promise I won't do anything bad ever again."

He washes the glass out of my cuts. I'm crying, and I tell him it hurts. I look in his beautiful blue eyes and say, "This is what you do to people. This is what you do to *me.*"

The ambulance arrives. Jeremy gets into the back with me and explains everything to the paramedic. They're talking in French, and I'm so drunk that I can't understand anything. I'm reduced to this, a crying mess like I'm back in my first year here.

The ambulance guy is hot, though, and I want to fuck him. He takes me to the ER while Jeremy stays behind. It's five a.m., and I have to wait for hours, alone, without Jeremy, while my hand bleeds. Finally I see a doctor who, as he stitches the needle through my knuckle, tells me that I really need to slow down before something even worse happens. "I know," I say. When I stumble home, the sun is out.

I have to keep a white bandage on my hand for days and can masturbate only with my right hand, which feels really weird, so I switch to my left before the stitches are taken out, before the cut is healed, not realizing that I'm creating a permanent scar. When the stitches are removed, there is a scar down my knuckles. I fall asleep for a whole day and wake up with my body aching.

Sober this time, I walk to Jeremy's apartment because he won't return my calls. "I'm so sorry. Like you wouldn't believe. But I need to know if you forgive me, if we'll still be friends."

"Look, Arthur. Just give me a few days. I need some time. But I forgive you, and you wanna know why? Because I understand you. It doesn't mean I agree with you, with how you act sometimes. But I understand you. You're one of the most emotional people I've ever met. It's okay. Don't beat yourself up over this because that will only make you feel worse than you already do. I know you feel bad, and I don't want you to feel worse. Just leave me alone for a few days."

*

It's my last winter in Montreal. I discovered that I got accepted into graduate school in New York. I tell Jeremy over the phone, and he sounds surprised that I now have to leave Montreal. We agree to meet downtown after work to celebrate. We go to a bar, order beers, and talk about the details of my getting into the school. After one beer, he starts to act goofy, like he's really buzzed. Maybe he's faking it, but he lets me kiss him while he sits on the bar stool, my tongue down his throat. It's the first time we've kissed in public in years. He spreads his legs apart, and I stand between them, my hands groping his ass while we make out like some newly-in-love couple. We have one more beer and then he asks me if I want to go to his place.

Back in his bed, we start to make out. We've been hooking up once in a while, so it's not a big deal, but in the middle of kissing me, he grabs my face, his eyes search mine, and he says, "Tell me you love me."

Without a moment's hesitation I say, "I love you," as if I'm confessing.

We start to kiss. He pauses and says, "Say it again."

"I fucking love you, Jeremy."

"I love you too," he says, and we continue to kiss and touch each other.

I say, "I've always loved you, you're mine," and fireworks go off in my head because he finally admitted he still loves me. We cum at the same time. I fall asleep holding him, kissing the back of his neck. It's the first time in ages that he lets me spend the night at his place, in the same bed. I fall asleep in minutes, so happy to have my arms around him, thinking, *This is it, we'll figure it out, then he'll move to New York with me, and we will make it work.*

*

It's a week before the move, and Jeremy is standing in my apartment. Last night, he told me he wants to come with me.

"We can just get married, and then I'll be able to come with you," he says sounding excited.

"Okay. But does this mean we'll be back together?" There is an awkward pause.

"No," he says. "We'd just be like ... how we are now, how we've been. We'd live together, but we'd still date other people."

"What the fuck would the point of that be? You want to move to another city with me but *still* not be back with me? What do I have to do for you to get it? I'm telling you that I would stick around forever, given the chance. I don't want to build that with some other random person who I happen to meet when we are both at the right age for it, the right mindset, you asshole! I want it with you. I know I want it, right now. What are you holding out for? What are you waiting for?"

The room grows silent. The light in the kitchen, a solitary bulb with no shade around it casts a grinding glare over everything. It is proof that I can't keep a home yet, can't keep things clean, can't be alone. Jeremy stands across the room from me but feels farther away. He throws his arms up and then slams them down—I never see him make emotional gestures—and he yells, "Of course I want those things too! Yes, I want those things with you! But when I'm, like, fucking thirty years old! I can't think about that right now—it's too much pressure! I want it with you, but when I'm older and ready for that."

For a few minutes, I don't say anything.

"But you do want them."

He nods. That's all I need for the moment.

"If you know you want those things with me," I say, "then why the fuck do you care about other people? It's like caring what some random fucking tourist thinks of you, if he wants to fuck you or not when he visits again. Why do you search for this validation that you don't need from people like that? What are you looking for that I can't give you?"

He starts to tear up a little. "Because I know you love me, but I want someone else to love me for once!" He's shouting now. "I want someone else to think I'm fucking beautiful! Think about our lives ever since we've been broken up, Arthur. You get *anyone* you want! You have a crazy life, you throw people out for the stupidest reasons! How many people have been interested in me since we broke up compared to you? I just want someone else to love me. No one has fallen for me except for you."

"So why isn't that enough? My love, my admiration?" I ask, unable to resist.

Of course, there is no answer to that question.

He sniffles. "Come on," he says. "I don't know."

*

Jeremy and I are doing a shoot with my photographer friend. We're dressed up to look like angelic church boys, decked out in pastel colours. We both wear white button-downs with light-blue vests, rosaries dangling out of the pockets, and violet handkerchiefs. We sit and make expressionless faces while being photographed, our arms intertwined so that the viewer can't tell whose is whose. It's the first time we've touched in weeks.

*

Despite all of the confusion between us, he still spends the night sometimes. When we wake up in the morning, we look our worst, which is my favourite—the horrible bedhead hair, the vulnerability. We're so used to it that it's not awkward. This morning it's almost like we're boyfriends again. Jeremy is wrestling with me, slapping me in a goofy way and calling me a dummy. He sprays me with Febreeze, and I'm in a cloud of mist. I'm laughing, happy.

I notice something when I look at photos of me and him from the past few years.

I never, ever smile the way I do when I'm around him.

*

In a dream, he looks exactly like my best friend from grade school—same smile, same hair colour. In a dream, our lines alternate between *Please don't leave me* and *I have to leave* and *I can't do this anymore*, except the dialogue takes place in a snowstorm, and I can't tell who is saying what.

*

Tu sais, tu arrives dans une nouvelle ville et tu ne connais personne, pas du tout. Tu ne parles pas la langue de cette ville-là. Et maintenant tu parles la langue d'ici mais les gens vont dire que ta langue est broken. *Mais tu peux le parler. Et tu adores. Et maintenant que tu parles la langue, toutes les portes s'ouvrent, même l'esprit de la ville auquel, avant, tu n'avais pas accès. Les gens que tu rencontres, les gens avec qui tu tombes en amour, ils disent des choses à toi comme: tu es américain, tu ne vas jamais, jamais comprendre la vie ici, il n'y a aucune raison de prendre notre vie ensemble ici au sérieux car quand tu auras fini tes études, tu partiras comme tous les autres, comme un câlice de touriste. Ce sera impossible pour toi de te faire une vie ici, une vraie vie. "Mais je veux me faire une vie ici," dis-je en anglais, mais non, ce sera pas possible—tu travailleras dans un centre d'appel toute ta vie si tu restes ici. C'est pourquoi on ne pourra jamais devenir vieux ensemble. On sait tout de suite que notre temps est limité. Limité par la nationalité, limité par la langue, l'éducation, l'argent, l'immigration, l'âge. "Nous vivons un amour impossible." Moi et toi, moi et la ville.*

Mais je vais faire l'effort!

Ça ne sert à rien. Laissez-faire, Arrête. C'est fini.

Mais maintenant je parle! Maintenant on parle la même langue. Je vais faire de l'argent. Je gagne ma vie. On pourrait vivre ensemble.

Non! J'ai dit non, câlice!

Maintenant que c'est possible, tu dis non encore!

Oui! Je suis encore jeune! Il ne faut pas que tu attendes! Je te donnais des raisons avant, des excuses, mais c'était seulement des histoires! Notre histoire, c'était une histoire, chéri! Et maintenant, tu veux fixer tout ça, tu cherches des solutions comme toujours. La réponse c'est encore non. Chui trop jeune, tu me stresses.

Kess tu veux que j'fasse, Jeremy. C'est impossible pour moi de savoir si je suis en amour avec toi ou en amour avec Montréal. C'est la même chose.

*

It's one of my last nights in Montreal, and Jeremy and I are climbing to the top of the Mountain to see the skyline. It's pitch-black except for the city lights and our puffs of breath. We stare at the revolving city searchlight that sits on the top of the tallest building and searches over the city like a beacon. I've seen that light every night for the past five years.

I look at Jeremy. "Whenever I saw that light flash over the city, I imagined it was searching for something. I always felt like that light. Searching for something in the night." *You see a flashing light and you think you are that flashing light.*

Jeremy smirks. "Did you find what you were looking for?"

"I think I found every goddamn thing I could here."

"Found, but couldn't keep."

"Well, not yet, anyway. I'm better at searching for things than that light, don't you think? They should put me up there. That's why I have to leave."

*

In my last days here, Jeremy meets me at a café and gives me a pink plastic ball that he found in the streets of the gay village, one that fell from the strings of pink balls strung over Rue Saint-Catherine. "It's raining pink balls."

*

All of August
caught between
The K holes, babe
the ketamine

You my dear
you finer thing
You my dear
my vitamin

*

In the backyard of your mother's house. In your high-school bedroom. In my best friend's bed at a house party. In the shower of my anarchist commune apartment, two a.m., loudly. You bled a little. In my summer sublet apartment. In the apartment after that. In your residence. In front of your best friend. In the fucking tiny one-person shower. In the living room. On the Internet. In the living room at your mother's house. On the furniture. With swords and fun rape-roleplay. Called you "Tommy."

On the kitchen floor of your mother's house. Tracing your cum stains across my bedsheets. It's a history, a constellation. With my mind. With your beauty. With other people. With the lights on. With a condom on—don't you ever do it without, or I'll find him and kill him. In the bedroom of your best friend for no good reason. In the chalet in the countryside, in the shower when you washed my hair slowly, the soap suds and sun in my eyes. How stupid of me to feel okay and I remember it now how slowly your hands were moving, thinking about the end.

And then, in your new apartment bedroom; afterward you slept on the couch. And then, in your apartment again in the living room, on the kitchen floor. I came over to do laundry, your bedroom again and again you on the couch. We can sleep together, but we can't sleep together. You stare at me while I smoke my cigarette, and I wonder why. You tell me I'm a nine out of ten, but you won't sleep in your own bed if I'm there, and then. Stoned, drunk, or hungover. In love and out of love but always with love. Asking if you consent to cuddling. On the phone. In the time that has passed when we say, "I have a staggering amount of mismatched socks from boys I don't recall."

Sixty-nine or on your knees. How it doesn't always come down to up ... the ass. In English *comme en français*. During the pause of a photoshoot while we're dressed up to look like saints. In the washroom of a resto in the southwest. In the hallway, almost, you rock-hard in my palm despite your boyfriend, you spun around, up against the wall before your roomie stopped us from cumming at the same time, forever, send me floating home through the air, lover—with your sentence

like a song
in my head:

"It will never be finished between us,
so don't worry about the end."

PART 3

this could be mine

I take a rideshare from Montreal to New York with only a suitcase packed. I get out at Penn Station and make my first trek to Brooklyn. Compared to Montreal, the place, the scenery is downright depressing, shocking, and confusing. I have to readjust to outright capitalism.

A few days into it, jobless, I go to meet Jason. In his black-and-white online photo, he's innocent and cute. At this point, I know that must be a lie. He's the same age as me. I googled his phone number and found out that he's an escort. When I meet him, I can see why he makes good money selling sex. I smoke cigarette after cigarette around him and fret about finding a job and how stupid it was to move to NYC with minimal savings.

*

Am I really that susceptible that I can fall in love over the smell of your cologne or the smell of your laundry detergent? Your armpits? Shouldn't I hold your actions to the same standards? And what then, if I did? I wish your words had scent.

*

"We're not so different, you and I."

*

Jason and I hang out and fuck a few times but I figure nothing major is happening. He said he's into some other guy, so I take it for what it is. I'm too strung out over leaving Jeremy to have real feelings for anyone right now anyway, although I have to admit the ease with which Jason has casual sex sleepovers is unsettling, even to me. I run into him on the street while he's with the other guy, Liam, a model, and Jason invites me to come bowling with them, to join their little date, and I say no, thanks. Liam has no idea that a week ago, I fucked the guy he's with. As soon as I see Jason out with Liam, I figure, fuck it, nothing is really happening here. And I'm busy getting into New York.

A few weeks later, I get an online message from Jason telling me that he's moving to Europe. He says that things didn't work out between him and Liam so he's running off to Europe with some rich older guy. Jesus, how retro. I didn't think guys still did this. Why not just be poor? Why not just wait tables? But then I get another message from him not even two weeks later:

Hey,

The guy I moved to Barcelona with turned out to be crazy. He was supposed to set me up with a job in his company but it didn't happen. So I'm fleeing Barcelona with almost no money. I am en route to Paris where I'll stay with a friend for a few days and then after maybe Berlin. I don't know. My life is a mess. I miss you a bit.

xo, Jason

I'm a tiny bit skeptical that it's "the guy" who turned out to be nuts, rather than the boy who ran off to Europe with him at a whim, but whatever. I'm glad I had the foresight not to get attached, because he'll be in Europe for a while.

Still, I miss him a little. He helped me adapt to how New York is more cut-throat, more individualistic, is fueled by money and good looks plus coke and alcohol. I miss the community and solidarity that I associate with Montreal. I decide to go to the club that Jason used to take me to, where we felt on top of Manhattan, where I felt poor and rich at the same time. It's weird being there without him but also liberating. Being here without him reminds me that this world exists independently of him, and I can do whatever I want. Whoever I want.

On the main floor all I can smell is the chlorine from the pool. I love that smell, and it's mixed with the music, the models, the champagne. It almost smells like bleach, which makes the place seem impeccably clean, the polar opposite of the dive bars and underground parties I'm used to. From across the dance floor, I can see a very tall boy with brown hair and striking features. He keeps smiling at me. He wears a blue blazer with a white button-down underneath, looking very classy. After a couple of whiskeys, I gather up the courage to ask him his name.

"Liam," he says. "And you're Arthur, right?"

"Yeah," I say, stunned. "How did you know? I just moved here."

"I met you with Jason. Once on the street, once at a party. He talked about you."

"Oh, you're *Jason's* Liam!"

"Well, not anymore."

Jason is far enough away that I guess it doesn't really matter that this guy has been making eyes at me all night. Winter is approaching, and any new friend in New York is a good friend. So I leave the party with Liam, who is a Swedish boy in New York solely for the purpose of modelling. He doesn't treat it like a big deal, and while he is obviously stunning, so are a lot of other people. In fact, I've come to realize, there's some kind of tipping point of physical beauty. It's not like the first or even second time you go out with someone you find impossibly gorgeous, when it's all new and you feel lucky to have them. At a certain point, it doesn't matter, and the standard can't be pushed any further. I am curious about Liam, though. Jason was infatuated with him, so I figured there must be something there. The possibility that Jason only liked him for being beautiful was beyond my grasp. I'd never met someone that shallow before.

We're outside, at the subway stop that will take us in opposite directions, him toward East Harlem and me back to Brooklyn.

"Whatever happened with you and Jason?" I ask, trying to figure out if the broken love triangle we're about to start is good to go.

He hesitates. "We'd been seeing each other for a while, and I thought he was a very good guy, but he knew that I had a boyfriend back in Sweden, and I guess he thought I was going to break up with this boy for him, but I couldn't do it. One night, he just flipped out on me, and he said some very mean things, the meanest things anyone's ever said to me. He sent me lots of text messages just attacking me. He was acting crazy. He was like a completely different person, or I had seen a side of him that he'd hidden before."

I can tell he is having trouble expressing himself. His English is okay but limited. He asks me what happened with Jason and me.

"Nothing, really. We just saw each other a few times. It was all pretty light-hearted, although I did notice sometimes that if I didn't do what he said, he'd get really cocky and rude, then I'd call him on it, and he'd stop. He seems like a nice enough guy, but comes off a bit arrogant. I'm new to the city, so I figured I can't be too picky. I just want someone to hang out with."

"Me too," Liam says. "It doesn't have to be some big dramatic thing."

With that, we exchange numbers. Soon after, we start dating.

*

I pass most of the winter with Liam, much like I had with Matthieu, and it is much the same. He is sweet. He reminds me of boys I loved in the past. He is always nice, he cooks, he buys me little presents, he is agreeable—all around a good guy, and god, so insufferably boring. I can't discuss anything with him that goes beyond the here and now. I try to open his mind, but it is too late. All he can talk about is the things that happen to him during the day. He can talk about modelling. When I try to talk about art or life with him—anything abstract, complex, adult—he just says things like, "It'll all be okay!"

But I want to at least discuss how to get to the point of it all being okay. He floats through existence. He is physically perfect but lacks intrigue. I miss the complexities and neuroses, all the interesting parts of past lovers. I miss Jeremy's slightly too big goofy ears, Phil's weird angelic blank stare, Fred's fucked-up country-bumpkin teeth, hell, even Jason's snaggletooth. Maybe boys are prettier when they have a flaw.

Still, I enjoy the social prestige of being with Liam. People would come up to us at parties just to say hi and ask how long we've been dating. I've been in New York for only two months, and already people are gossiping about us. It gives me a kind of ego boost, so I can only imagine how high that must have made Jason. I could feel myself getting sucked into the kind of shallow, New York bullshit that Jason seemed to worship, and I wanted nothing to do with it. Besides, even though it's slightly surreal being with Liam—walking around the city with him and then seeing his face on a huge H&M billboard—after a while, I realize that it's just an image. He's a person, not a personification, and behind closed doors, when the prestige doesn't matter, it's still his personality that's most important. If Michelangelo could have brought David to life and had to put some clothes on him and date him for a few months, maybe he wouldn't have idolized him so much.

It gets to a point where Liam and I are de facto boyfriends and I have feelings for him the way someone has feelings for the cute guy you see in the subway station but then never see again. I knew it had no long-term potential from the beginning, so it never gets deep. I don't like this new me—almost impenetrable, emotionally hardened. One night in bed, I tell Liam that I think we should just be friends, that we don't have very much in common. He seems shocked, but acts like he agrees. We kiss each other goodbye in the morning and act like everything is fine, normal, that we'll be friends and just see each other less. We never see each other again. He moves away from New York a year later.

*

I take a rideshare to Montreal because I miss it there. I miss the vibe and energy, the feeling of togetherness. I miss the way French feels coming off my tongue. I miss the multi-coloured architecture, the apartments in the Plateau. But mostly I miss Jeremy. We've been staying in touch since I moved, which is good and bad for me. We can't let go, can't move forward. I feel trapped by staying in touch with him, like I'm emotionally tethered to this one possibility, but the thought of no longer being in each other's lives doesn't appeal to either of us. I must like the pain of being addicted to a person like this. Whenever I get drunk at the bar I work at in New York, I send him ridiculous text messages about how I want to marry him. He just brushes it off.

When I get to Montreal, I have to go out to the suburbs to meet Jeremy at his parents' place. Around the same time that I move to New York, he moves back in with his parents. Poetic tragedy. But his life wasn't going anywhere, so he decides to move home, save money, and reapply to school. At the same time, he finds a new boyfriend—another guy with dark hair, dark eyes, and tattoos. Whatever. I give it a few months, at best. The new guy doesn't know that I'm going to see Jeremy, of course.

As soon as I get there, it all starts to flood back—the summer we fell in love, years ago, and how nice his family was to me. They still are. I have a cigarette with

Jeremy's mom on the patio.

"I don't know why we're still friends," I admit to her.

"I understand it can be confusing at your age," she says.

"He almost moved with me, you know."

"I know. He called me a few days after you found out you were accepted to graduate school. He told me, 'I think I'm falling back in love with Arthur.' I wasn't surprised, to be honest. You boys met when you were too young. And then, all of a sudden, a few days later, he said that he was just upset and confused because you were leaving."

Jeremy and I hang out down in his basement bedroom where we first fell in love. It's almost like nothing has changed. His mother calls him upstairs, and he tells me that he'll be right back. As soon as he's gone, I search the room for a pair of his dirty underwear to jerk off to. I find a pair of boxers that have the smell of his dick and ass all over them. I go into the bathroom next to his room—we used to fuck in here—and lock the door. I press the underwear up to my face, inhaling the remnants of his scent, and start to stroke myself, thinking of his hole, thinking of when he used to be mine, my fucking boy. All gone now—miss him, miss him, need it still. Minutes go by. He's taking too long to come back down, on purpose. There's a slow knock on the bathroom door. Fuck it. He knows what I want to do. I come out of the bathroom with a sheepish grin, toss the underwear back into the dirty laundry pile, and lie down on the bed.

"I knew you were going to do that," he says.

"I knew that you knew."

"Well, did you at least get to finish?"

"No. Can I finish?"

"You might as well," he says. "I mean, since you already started."

"What about your boyfriend?"

"I'm not actively participating in anything. I'm just saying you can finish."

So I lie there on his bed, five years later, pull down my jeans, and continue to jerk myself. He watches, hesitant and horny. Eventually, on the other side of the bedroom, he drops his pants too, but keeps his boxers on, stroking himself through the boxers. We watch each other jerk off, like two boys in freshmen year.

"This is ridiculous," I tell him.

"I can't do anything," he says.

So I go over to him just to stand there, closer, touching, jerking. I get down on my knees in front of him. I press my face up against his cotton boxers, his fist and cock inside. I tell him to turn around. I put my face into his sweet little candy-ass—his boxers still on—and take a deep sniff. *Fuck*, it still gets me every time. He strokes himself inside his boxers, while behind him, I sniff his hole and jerk off. I can smell all of the grime and sweat, the boyishly dirty smell of his ass. His dick throbs from how turned on he is from being worshipped like this. He presses his ass back, hard against me, grinding his hole into my face. I pull the boxers down, and we keep going, his ass cheeks now completely engulfing my face, my nose buried in his hole, lapping up the scent. I can't hold back any longer, so while I grind my face into his ass, I give him a few good wet laps with my tongue, and with that we both cum in a dizzying few seconds. After we wipe up, we pull up our pants. The smell of his asshole is still all over my face. This chemistry is the reason I hang on. If you want to know how attracted you are to someone after a few years, try to get off by just inhaling their smell.

There is a weird feeling in the air, though—guilt, regression—and he's just sort of cheated on the new guy. The intensity we've experienced brings us even closer, acting as a kind of undeniable proof that whatever there is between us isn't finished. So when I ask if I can spend the night, like I had spent the night there so many times before, and although I promise not to tell the new guy, his answer is "No." He says it'd be too weird, but I can tell he wants me to.

I take the last night bus out of the suburbs, with the smell of him still all over me. That is the last time I'd see him at his parents' house, where I'd imagined a life of seeing his family during holidays, of being, well, related. Those are just memories now, longings I have to drop off somewhere, while his smell on my face gradually diminishes.

*

It hardly snows in New York that winter, but the morning Liam leaves it starts to snow. Spring is approaching, but someone has stolen my jacket at a nightclub. Being broke in New York is nothing like being broke in Montreal.

I get a message from Jason while he's still in Europe. He finds out that Liam and I have been dating. The message says, "By the way, we aren't friends. I know what your game is." What a creepy paranoid fuck. My game? I didn't even know who Liam was at first, when I approached him a few months ago. It's not like I was in some kind of BFF position with Jason that we wouldn't date each other's exes. When Jason gets back to NYC, he messages me to apologize. I'm skeptical, but he says he was just hurt over Liam not being with him and that he took his pain out on me. I think of what Liam told me about Jason flipping out on him and going nuts. Apparently it was bad enough that Liam never wanted to speak to Jason again, so there is definitely something dangerous there.

I'm not sure about Jason. In a way—and he points this out—we don't really know each other at all. We've hung out a few times having casual sex and watching cartoons, and we've gone together to parties a few times. I'd felt a bit disposable around him. I wonder if that's how people feel around me, too. Jason introduces me to people as his "poet friend," which makes me feel like an accessory. I also hold him in contempt—something I think he is not used to—for not having anything going on for himself besides his good looks. It is clear that we have a lot of differences. And yet, he's asked me to hang out again. I'm still in desperate need of companionship, so I agree to join him for drinks and a night out. At his apartment, I see his roommate Sofia, who I haven't seen in months, and she says to me, "Well, well, well, look who it is. I knew you'd be back, my dear."

Out on the rooftop overlooking Manhattan, Jason and I are slightly drunk and decide to talk it out. He explains that he was upset because he felt like I stole Liam from him. I tell him that it really had nothing to do with him. I can intuit that this is hard for him to wrap his head around—the idea of something having nothing to do with him. Then we start talking about us—whatever the fuck that is. He says I never showed much interest.

"All you would ever do," I say, "is text me to come over, 'hang out,' and fuck. You never asked me to, like, actually go and do anything with you. It was always a whim. You never talked to me about anything, you never told me anything about yourself."

He looks confused. "But you never asked."

"I never asked because you never gave me the impression that you wanted me to care about those things. As soon as we met, you put me in fuck-buddy zone because you were into Liam."

"That's true," he says. "We should try to actually get to know each other. I think you'll find that I have a lot to offer ..."

It's spring, and nothing else is going on for me, so I decide to take him up on his offer. We leave the nightclub, go out into the street past the dealers muttering "molly, coke," and back to the West Village. On the walk back to his place, I try to map out in my head where the nearest subway station is, but before I can, he asks me to spend the night. I tell him that I think it's a really bad idea because I'm drunk, but he pleads and says we'll just cuddle. He stops me in the middle of the sidewalk, starts making out with me, and it's all so fucking romantic in a depleted kind of way, so I say, "Okay, fine."

When we get to his place, his bedroom seems familiar, and any sense of familiarity feels good to me. We lie down and start to cuddle and spoon. He tries to fuck me, but I say, "No." He reminds me that I used to fuck him in the fall and never let him fuck me, which isn't really fair. If we want new beginnings, we have to try new things. I'm a little bit drunk and he does have a point, so I agree. He puts a condom on—after some convincing—holds my legs up in the air, and rims me to get me wet, which he's unnervingly good at. He slowly pushes his dick into me with my legs over his shoulders. I haven't been fucked in a long time, but his dick isn't super thick so it doesn't hurt; in fact, it's just the right size. He pushes in and out and makes eye contact with me the whole time, which is hot. I can tell he is getting off on the whole idea of fucking another top—the conquest, the invasion. I struggle a bit and say "ow," which I can tell turns him on. He ends up being as good at it as he promised. He has great rhythm and force, and when he's inside me, his dick creates a constant orgasm effect. I see a new side of him while he's fucking me: Jason the rent boy transforms into Jason the dominant and masculine. As a bottom, he used to just lie there like a dead fish, and I never saw him as powerful, despite his broad shoulders. And I feel powerless yet stronger when he's inside me.

Afterward, we fall asleep next to each other, not really cuddling. When we wake up, things aren't awkward, which is a relief. I say, "See you later," when we part, leaving it open-ended, thinking we'll be fuck friends again. I don't expect anything serious from him.

Over the next few days, he starts to text me and call me a lot, give me attention and invite me to hang out. It feels like he's being considerably nicer than before. He actually seems to give a fuck about my life, so I open up to him, a tiny bit anyway, something I otherwise don't allow myself to do in New York. I open up without thinking about how being passively loved tends to make me open up. I start to tell him about all the stuff that casual lovers don't talk about: creative projects, exes, how graduate school is going, or how someone stole my jacket at a nightclub. When he hears this, he invites me over to his place and lets me borrow a jacket. It's from a friend of Sofia's. He gives me free clothes because he says I have to cut it out with my "teenage grungy punk rock bullshit" and that I'm "too pretty" for all of "this artsy Brooklyn shit." I resent that. I tell him that I'm actually sort of broke and that, like a lot of artists, I live this way so that I have maximum free time to pursue my creative interests. Jason thinks that's stupid; why don't I escort, like him, and make a bunch of money? I explain to him that the bourgeois epoch is on the way out, that there is no sense investing in a bankrupt capitalist society. He laughs at me and tells me I'm ridiculous. He'd rather be on the side of the rich when the so-called revolution comes. It pisses me off but intrigues me.

I take the train home in the morning from his apartment in the West Village to my apartment in deep Bushwick to find that the door has been kicked in by my roommate in what is doubtless another drunken, fucked-up alcohol haze. I see that the upstairs door is busted in too, along with the glass. The mice I can handle, even as they scurry across the mattress on the floor, but in the past few weeks, the roommate's drinking and coke binges have gotten out of hand. Just then, he walks by and says, "I don't wanna talk about it."

Later that day, I take some photos of the damages and send them to Jason. I need to move out, and I tell him that I want to look for a new room. Jason offers a simpler solution.

"Just move in with me," he says. "Sofia won't mind." He says I can come stay with him for as long as it takes to find a new place.

"But we just started talking again a week ago. Isn't it kind of weird?"

"It's only weird if you make it weird. I like having you around, and you clearly need to get out of there. Plus, I sort of get off on helping people. I'm a very giving person."

I'm hesitant because I've never lived with a guy who I was involved with, but I have to get out of there. I spend the next few nights at his place. One night, we go back to my apartment—luckily, the cokehead roommate is in the shower and the other one isn't home—gather up all my stuff, and hail a taxi. Jason tells me afterward that he pepper-sprayed all the doorknobs in the apartment.

"Why the fuck would you do that?"

"Just to do it. They fucking deserve it!"

In a city of eight million people, it feels good to have one on your side, even if he seems a little crazy.

*

I've been living with Jason while trying to find a new place. It's surprisingly nice; I feel very adult, like we've instantly become a mature couple. We're getting closer to each other, but we avoid talking about what it means, which is fine by me. Simultaneously, I've told Jeremy that I don't want to speak to him anymore. I say that I can't be "just friends" because I will always want more from him. He acts confused and says it's fucked up. I feel guilty, but being friends with him is keeping me from falling in love with anyone else. He still texts me, but I've just stopped replying. This was Jason's idea. He tells me that I have to cut Jeremy out, completely. That the kid is just keeping me around as a backup and that there is no point in hanging on to him. Every time Jeremy tries to contact me, I ignore him, even though my heart cracks when I think of it. But it works. The more I ignore Jeremy, the less I feel caught up in my love for him.

Jason takes this to mean, somehow, that I'm into him on a romantic level. I've been living with him for about a week when he asks me very calmly, "Do you want to be my boyfriend?" I don't quite believe him—he acts like such a player all the time. Part of me wants to say yes, because here is a gorgeous guy lying in bed half-naked, asking me to be his boyfriend. But what would happen? Even if I do have feelings for him, he will eventually break my heart. He's just asking me; it's not like he's really done anything to warrant boyfriendhood. I'm not going to say yes just because he's cute and we're sleeping together. He'd just dump me when he gets bored. I know the type. Hell, I've been the type.

"But Jason, I don't really have emotions for anyone at the moment. I really appreciate all your help and you letting me live with you, but we don't really have common values, do we? I mean, the sex is great, don't get me wrong, but we disagree about pretty much everything."

"But none of that really matters," he protests vaguely, falsely.

"Don't take this the wrong way, but I don't really see the point in calling anyone my boyfriend unless it's really serious." What I mean to say is, "I'm a hard-core radical romantic poet, and you're a bourgeois, morally bankrupt rent boy who only gives a fuck about status and money, and you hardly ever act sincere or genuine," but I have to be tactful. I know it's driving him crazy that for once, a boy isn't stumbling all over him, grateful just to be in his presence and gaze at his pretty-boy face. He isn't used to dealing with a "bad boy rebel type" (which he likes to call me; I'll go with it) who doesn't kiss his ass and actually calls him out on his bullshit. If he really likes me, I figure, I'll give it a while, let him work for it, prove it. I like him a little bit, of course, but I don't trust him just yet.

"Okay," he says, sounding disappointed. "But then, can we at least be kind-of boyfriends?"

I like the verbal modification, so I agree. I like the thing between us lately, and I am getting attached. I think it's cool that we both feel that monogamy is only necessary in certain circumstances, that he's not afraid to deviate from the norm. Even though he comes off as shallow in public, around me, he's getting comfortable. He has a bit of a tummy (points for not being a gym-nazi body fascist), and he's letting the hair on his chest and shoulders get unruly. I can tell he isn't used to letting his guard down around someone, and it's sexy to watch. Not that I am particularly fond of hairy guys, but I am fond of realness, and I love seeing someone who acts so fake at parties gradually become a real human being around me. Getting all hairy and gross. I'm even starting to like the way his doggy boy-breath smells in the morning. *Oh shit, maybe I should have just said yes ...*

And the sex. Fuck, the sex.

*

"You're my good little cleaner boy, and you have to do what I say or else I'll have to punish you."

"Oh, come on, Jason, not now. I'm not in the mood. We can't do it up here anyway. I'm sure there are cameras."

"We can do whatever I want. You're being a bad boy. I'm paying you, so you have to do what I say. Now take off your pants."

"I really don't think it's a good idea to get into this up here ..."

He unbuckles my belt and bends me over the sofa. "Shh. Just be a good boy and do what I say."

We're in one of the most expensive jewellery boutiques in the Upper East Side. He's dressed in clothes that cost more than my monthly rent. So finally I play along.

"Yes, sir, whatever you say, sir."

He spreads my ass cheeks apart as I kneel on the sofa and tells me I'm a good cleaner boy, pressing his tongue up to my asshole. He asks me if I like that, and I say, "Uh-huh. Yes, sir." I can control him like this too. He thinks he controls me, but I control him through desire. I let him fuck me, sure, but he can't have me—not completely. Not yet.

He rims me into ecstasy on the sofa, then whips out his dick and pokes it into me raw. I moan and say "Fuck" and "Ah, man" and "Fuck me, I've been a bad boy," and he says, "Yeah, cleaner boy, be a good boy and take my dick." I give up my ass to him and let him pound me, trying not to cum before he does, which is a challenge. I can feel him going faster and then slow down, so I cum in my palm, careful to not drip anywhere. Every time he cums in me, I'm scared, but I love how addicted to it he is, it's *me* he has to cum in, saying things like, "I haven't had an ass like yours in a while."

*

We keep getting into fights over bareback sex. He tells me that if we can't fuck raw, then we have to stop fucking altogether. I tell him that it's not safe and ask why it's such a big deal. Why can't we just use condoms?

"Because I use condoms when I'm working. Not with people I'm into."

*

A snaggletooth grin hooks
The lip. They gotta pay to play.

Cute and cocky. You play hookie.
It's the look in the looking

That we like—what about that one,
Or that one. It's the feeling of falling

That I like. You're growing fond of me
In your bed, it's the warmth of the flesh

That creates this illusion. I'm old
Enough to know. Hold me now I'm broke

and weak. A vagabond, bandit, bambi. An iamb
out of pentameter. *A barback*. You like that word

With an e between r & b. Senseless and begging
me. *Safe with all the others.* Adding this to my list

Of things that maximize pleasure. It's the fucking
Feeling of the fleeting that I love, the crush

Without the crash. It's their cash
That makes you hard. I'm cruising

on control. I think I'm funny like the night
Sofia was passed out in your bed.

I'm going home, she said, walking into
Your closet. You already are home.

Too many Geminis in this house, Sofia says.
Be nice. You bicker like a married couple, you silly

faggots. Hold me don't hold me. I want to be in love
When really I'm longing for more lonely.

*

Jason comes to Brooklyn (a rarity) to see my new place. We're going over the elevated train across the East River, sharing a pair of earbuds. He sings "Piece of My Heart," and I just roll my eyes at him like he's nuts. He's sort of a jerk to me half the time, but then acts like he's in love with me and that I should somehow "know this" without him saying it. But he won't fucking say it, so I won't either.

*

Do I want to come over or do I not want to come over? Do I want to fuck or do I not want to fuck? Gradually, Jason starts to use these decisions against me. They are decisions that change the entire course of the relationship.

It has been a few weeks since he gave me that jacket, since he started to be really nice. Now he is acting like a dick, and I don't really get it. I keep saying to him, "Hey, if you want to be my boyfriend, things have to be sweet for a bit, and then we'll be together."

"No, it doesn't work that way with me. I can be nice to someone once they're mine, but otherwise they'll get treated like a cheap trick."

"Isn't that quite the opposite of how it's supposed to be?" I ask. "Aren't you doing everything in reverse? Like, you want something without having to work for it, and then you're basically throwing a fit when you don't get it."

He texts me a lot, demands that I come over. He's got a very controlling vibe. And when I tell him that I caved and started talking to Jeremy again, he says, "I knew it, and things were going so well before that."

I want to say, "Things weren't going at all. Nothing has changed, and it has nothing to do with you ..."

Jason has started to get abusive, but I just think of this as his machismo or some kind of fucked-up hard-core honesty. I justify it with the idea that an artist lives intensely. It's two a.m., and he wants to fuck. I'm honestly fucked out, so I say no. Jason tells me that if I can't fuck, then I need to leave. I sit up and look at him and say, "You wonder why I don't want to be with you."

"Well, if you really wanted to be with me, you would want to fuck all the time. It's not my fault you don't understand your own feelings."

"I understand my feelings perfectly. I just don't want to fuck at the moment."

"Then you can leave."

"Fine. I don't want to sleep next to you right now anyway. You're pissing me the fuck off, you're being an asshole. Ever since I told you I'm not ready for a relationship, you've been an asshole." I grab the jacket he gave me, and as I start to put it on, he grabs it from me, pulls it off me, and says, "I think you've had this for long enough."

"Seriously, Jason? It's March. It's the middle of the night. That's my only jacket. It's fucking cold out."

And without any remorse or sympathy at all he says, "You'll be fine."

"Wow, okay, fuck you." I leave.

The next day, he texts me: hi babe, did you have a nice walk last night? A bit chilly, huh?

*

Jason asks me to come over. I tell him I can't because I have to work on assignments for grad school, which is true.

"If you can't come over right now, you might as well fuck off for good. I don't want anything to do with you anymore."

"Babe," I say, "calm down. Why the fuck are you spazzing out?"

"Listen, I fucked plenty of boys raw this whole time I've been fucking you, so I don't really know if I'm negative or not." And with that, he hangs up.

I call him back repeatedly, and he answers but keeps hanging up. He lets hours go by before he tells me that he was joking and that "maaaaybe I took that one too far, but I love to feel you panic."

I call Jeremy and ask him if he would ever joke about that with someone. I tell him about all the sir and boy play and how, sure, it was all my idea sexually, but Jason does the powerplay thing out of bed too.

"You're asking me if I'd ever purposely, maliciously let someone think, for hours, that maybe I have HIV and maybe I gave it to them? If I would tell that to a lover as a kind of punishment for not wanting to fuck or come over or something?"

"Yeah. I mean I know it sounds crazy, but he gave me a gig and he helped me move when I was between places, you know ..."

"Arthur. It's a bait and switch. That guy sounds like a fucking psycho. You need to stop talking to him."

*

I decide to head back to Montreal to save money until the fall semester starts. I have to get away from Jason, and I'm running out of money. And I miss Montreal.

111

Jason says it's a bad idea, but what does he know? He's just a rent boy. He says I'm running away because I don't want things to get more serious between us, and, in a way, he's right. I don't want things to get more serious between myself and a guy who is such a fucking control freak, always taking my kinky S/M fantasies and putting them into practice outside the bedroom. Always flipping out on me and calling me a "bad friend" if I can't drop everything and come over right away. If I can't fuck one night, if I'm not in the mood, he'll kick me out of his apartment, then wonder why we aren't boyfriends. Yeah—I need to get away from him.

Back in Montreal, I live in a huge cheap apartment with a bunch of room-mates, and it's insanely relaxed compared to New York. I'm supposed to like this, but it only takes a little while before ... I notice how everyone acts like they're eighty years old compared to people in New York, and the only thing lower than the cost of living is people's level of ambition. Fuck, maybe Jason is right. Maybe everyone here is just a lazy hippie. I go back expecting that everything will be the same, but a lot of my old friends have gone to Europe for the summer. I hardly ever see Jeremy because he's still with his new boyfriend. A lot of the people I used to know don't really do much anymore. I'm back after being gone for almost a year and, well, no one cares. Every week that goes by I feel it stronger: I miss Jason, I miss Sofia, the parties, the high life, the ambition, the arrow pointed ever upward, the intensity.

But the move was based on economics: I needed to come back to save money. It's only for two-and-a-half months. I decide that Jason and I should continue not speaking for a little while longer because he was acting so out of control when I left. I get a text from him saying, "I'm drunk and I miss you." He says that he has feelings for me but doesn't know how to express them so he does things to piss me off, just to see if I have feelings too. How grown up.

Once every few weeks, I bike down to Jeremy's apartment and we have a secret hang-out, which means he's cheating on his boyfriend. It's been nearly five years since we met and we're still doing this. Back in the spring, when I was trying to shut him out, he texted me with a sob story about getting surgery. Of course I called him right away to make sure everything was okay (because who wouldn't?), but it turned out it wasn't a "serious" surgery, just a tactic to get me to respond.

When I called him, I was bawling and telling him how much I loved him because the word "surgery" conjured up scary thoughts.

It's become all too evident, throughout the summer, that this thing between me and Jeremy, whatever it is, has faded. We're not in sync when we talk to each other anymore. Jason was right: I left, I advanced. Although Jeremy's moved back to Montreal and is back in school and working a retail job, he's lost it, that spark. I never thought I'd see it happen. I don't even have to say anything about it because it's like he knows that he lost it and doesn't care.

I've watched too many of my muses die.

And now I miss New York, even though I sort of hate the place for exposing me to things that I was happier not knowing about. And I miss Jason, that crazy fuck.

＊

i searched for you
where the smoke plumes
loom in a luminous light
yes, like the moon.
i like the doom
of the night. i roamed
the tombs for you,
my wallflower, candyass,
pristine punk. how i sought
you out among the hairstyles
of the damned. in the east end
and back again. between
ecstasy and amphetamine.
you were *inspirant.* esperanto.
my abstract expressionist.

but there i found you

lacking flourish.
diminished, demure.
bathed in the hue
of a domestic decor,
dimmed by your candles,
burning at both ends.

*

I like it when we do this thing where he pins me down before he fucks me, puts his hands over my wrists like he's nailing them to the bed, and tells me to open my mouth. I like it when he tells me what to do. It's so much easier this way, so much easier to be shaped rather than having to shape someone and watch how badly they fail. I open my mouth and he spits into it. I mix his spit around with mine, smile, say "Mmm," and swallow.

Then he invades me and cums inside me. I'm his to take.

*

The first time that I bike down to Jeremy's place that summer, everything feels impeccably cool, like we haven't missed a beat. The TV is on in the living room, and the place is well-furnished. He's working at some tea-shop now, not doing too badly. Of course we get into it. He's being goofy the way he used to, and we smile at each other.

"You know we would be fine together," I say. "Tell me you wouldn't be happy with me in the long run, Jeremy. Please, just say it."

He hesitates. "How could it even work there?"

"We would split the rent that I pay for my bedroom. We would get married. That way, you could work or you could get student loans and finish school there. It's totally plausible."

"I'm with Antoine," he says.

"And if you weren't?"

"Yeah, we could be happy together."

"You're making it like this. You're making a choice. You know I'll always love you."

We go out on the porch and smoke a cigarette. Montreal feels like a dream that hasn't been discovered.

Inside, we sit on the couch, pretend to watch TV. Jeremy stands up to get something, but I reach out and put my arm around his waist, pulling his basketball shorts down, bending him over the sofa. Opening up old wounds to get a taste of him in bloom.

*

During the summer in Montreal, a friend decides to throw a club party and asks me to bartend. I agree to, since I'd done it in New York. I stand there shirtless, pouring vodka down the throat of any boy who wants it. Jeremy walks up to me. I haven't heard from him in weeks. Whenever he cheats on his boyfriend, he feels all guilty and disappears.

"Slut," he says flirtatiously. I glare at him.

"Where's Antoine?"

"I think he's at the other bar."

"Yeah? Well, I think I'm busy. I think you should join him."

After the party, I see him outside at the bus stop. I'm on my bike. "I bet I could make it back there before you can," I say to him. He just smiles.

I'm pretty drunk and not thinking, so I bike over there, and Jeremy reluctantly lets me inside.

"Arthur, it's really late, we shouldn't keep doing this. It makes me feel bad," he says while we're lying there in bed together.

"Okay. But please, at least just cuddle me. I've missed you so much."

While cuddling, I reach over and touch his cock to see if it's hard, and it is. "Ah-ha!" I say. I crawl on top of him and pin him down playfully, acting more drunk than I really am. I want to mess with him the way Jason would mess with me.

"You be a good boy. Do what I say," I tell him. He plays along a little bit—I roll him over and stick my face in his ass while he protests, as if I could hold him down with my arms on his lower back. I recall an old game of ours from years ago and say, "Come on Tommy, you be a good boy, I have your parents tied up in the other room, and if you don't do what I say, I will fuck you and then kill them."

"No, Arthur, come on. Seriously, we aren't doing this right now," he says.

"Bad Tommy." I continue to smother my face into his nylon silver basketball shorts, lapping up his boyish scent. "I'm gonna pound your boyhole, you sweet little twink bitch," I say to him with a menacing smile. He looks at me like I'm nuts. I wink. "Go with it," I say.

I turn him back over and pin him down, my knees across his biceps, take my cock out, and put it in his face. Jeremy says, "Ech!" and "I don't wanna! No!" while he's got a huge boner. He opens his mouth, and I jam it in a few times. I slap him somewhat hard across the face. He makes like he wants to keep his mouth shut, and I pinch his nostrils shut so that he is forced to open his mouth to breathe. He tells me that we really need to stop, that he really doesn't want to, and I still can't tell if he's just playing along until he grabs me, throws me off him, and tells me to leave.

"What's wrong?" I ask. "That was hot, wasn't it?"

"Yeah, and since when are you having sex that hard-core? I can't keep cheating on him," he says.

"You're such a fucking goddamn pussy, Jeremy," I say drunkenly. "You're standing there rock-hard, hard as fuck for me after five years, saying no because of your ridiculous new boyfriend, this Johnny-come-lately faggot with his tattoos, his black hair, Italian, Anglophone. What a joke. And Jason taught me to fuck like that—all out, all animal. We could go there too, but you hold yourself back, and not just sexually."

He says it's the last time we will ever fuck, but of course, he is wrong.

*

I figure it's about time to get therapy, but I can't afford it and I don't have the patience, so I decide I'll just take some mushrooms instead. I'm all alone in Montreal, and I figure taking them alone will be a good way to not freak out. It's a nice summer night, and I eat a few of them, wait for them to kick in.

They come on much stronger than expected, and suddenly I am in an ugly yellow sublet room, tripping and laying on a mattress on the floor—always with these goddamn mattresses on the floor—and I fixate upon the fruit flies in the room. My thoughts focus now on the themes of ROT, DECAY, and DEATH. I must strive to be a cleaner person, I realize. This is the first lesson learned. Grimes' music is freaking me the fuck out, so I decide I have to get up and leave the room, go outside, go for a bike ride.

While biking, everything starts to seem absolutely absurd. I'm glad to be alone so that no one else can see how weird this is. I am biking around the Plateau when I start to realize it, to feel it hard, the lesson, the theme of the trip. On one hand, I can't stop moving; I can't stop pedalling because my thoughts are behind me. On the other hand, if I don't stop moving, I'll never build anything.

Each apartment I pass by possesses its own history. I can hear, see, feel every door open. I catch glimpses of each person in each room and the history of each life. On the left-hand side of the street are authentic apartments, authentic lives, and on the right-hand side, off in the distance, are condo developments and cranes and plumes of dust or smoke. On one side of me is real life and on the other prefabricated construction. The empty unfinished buildings look desolate and bankrupt.

I get a text message from my dealer, but I am too high to reply. It dawns on me that I am alone, tripping, and Jeremy is off somewhere else. His story continues in another narrative. I am in awe at all the life around me, all the choices made, the choices to stay, to be somewhere. I think of everyone I know who has made the choice to either stay or leave. I could feel my own irrelevance, that little ego death that takes your self out of the picture. I mean, this whole time, I've been thinking of other people as ghosts drifting in and out of my love, but really, I'm the ghost, I'm the one drifting. The people in the apartments have put down roots. And Jeremy is out there somewhere, in an apartment, putting down roots. I could even go see him right now if I wanted to.

That's why the radiator in my room started to sing to me, *make a family, build a home, make a family, build a home.* And I said, *Ugh, radiator, you're being so moralistic and conservative, I'm outta here.* But maybe the radiator had a point.

I rest on my balcony as the trip winds down. Fucking mindfuck. Wasn't even fun. Still a little high, I have absolutely no one to talk to. To avoid feeling like a ghost, I take out my cell phone and text Jason: "High on shrooms alone in Montreal. Miss you."

He replies almost instantly: "Lol. Miss you too. See you soon when you get back."

A deep breath. Groundedness.

*

After my mushroom trip, I realize how totally alone I am, here or anywhere. I start to talk to Jason on a daily basis again. He tells me that he had a breakdown after I left New York and that during the entire spring, he tried to get me to stay. He tells me that, after I left, he went on a sex binge and let ten different guys come to his apartment and plow him. I'm still naïve enough to believe him. He says he wanted to feel completely destroyed. He's also informed me that he's quit his job at the boutique because he can make more money as an escort. I beg him not to quit, telling him that he's way more mentally stable with a normal job. "I'm hardly mentally stable anyway," he says. "It won't make that much of a difference."

A few days before I'm supposed to come back to New York, Jason messages me to ask when the next bus to Montreal leaves. "I have nowhere left to stay in New York and no more friends. I got kicked out of my sublet; the guy I was staying with called me a monster, broke up with me." I tell Jason that I'm exhausted; I've just finished a teacher training course. I'm supposed to go back to NYC in two days. Jason says maybe I'm not a good friend if I don't let him come to Montreal. He gets in at five a.m., walks through the apartment and into my bedroom. Even in my half-awake state, it strikes me as meaningful that, during this entire bullshit summer, Jeremy has never been to this apartment, not even once, and yet Jason is here from New York. He lies down in the bed next to me, still smelling like the cologne that I used to hate but now love. I'd forgotten how big and protective he feels, a solid twenty to thirty pounds heavier than me. He wraps his arms around me, we cuddle and go to sleep.

In the morning he is up, up, up and ready to go. He thinks he's on vacation. I try my best to show him a good time, but all he does is scoff at Montreal, while backhandedly saying that he can see why I like it so much considering where I came from. At night, I take him out to show him a good time, speaking with people in French most of the time because, uh, we're in Montreal, but Jason somehow manages to take offense at this. I take him out to a couple of different bars and clubs. He asks me where he can find ecstasy or ketamine. From across the dance floor of the club, he spots a group of young guys so he grabs my hand and leads me over to them. The one he likes is shorter and wearing a hoodie, and as we walk up, I realize it's Phil. I haven't seen him in years. Standing next to him is his boyfriend.

"You guys know each other?" Jason asks as we approach.

"Uh, yeah."

Phil and I awkwardly acknowledge each other and I introduce Jason. Out of Jason's earshot, I tell Phil that I still think about him sometimes. He gives me an unimpressed look and says, "*Deja deux ans et tu n'as rien oublie.*"

"How could I forget?" I ask him.

"*C'etais éphémère,*" he says.

"Ephemeral things have always been my favourite. That's the stuff poetry is made of."

"*Oui, parce que c'est celles qui laissent les meilleurs souvenirs, faute des temps pour voir les mauvais côtés des choses,*" he says, turning away.

At the end of the night, Jason begs me to go to a sauna with him, and I tell him absolutely not. He doesn't understand why. He fails to understand that this world he has entered is not make-believe for me. I walk my bike home because I'm too drunk to ride it—I figure Jason's gone to the sauna without me—when someone crashes into me from behind and I nearly fall over. I scream at him, "*What the fuck?!*" because he's hurt me, and this isn't the first time he's been too rough.

As we walk back to my apartment, he berates me and tells me that I'm a horrible host and I'm not letting him have any fun. I tell him to go fuck himself, that this kind of shit is the reason why we were never together in the first place—his failure to understand that the world does not revolve around him. I'm so mad at him that I let him sleep alone in my bed, and I go to sleep on the couch.

I wake up a few hours later. I'm still angry, but we fight like this so much that it holds little meaning. I go into my room and crawl into bed with him without saying anything. As soon as I lay down he puts his arm around me and holds me tight, which momentarily fixes everything. We don't have to say anything, we don't have to talk about it.

*

I go back to New York in the fall with a fresh perspective. I've left everything behind. I said goodbye to Jeremy a few days before leaving, and we talked on the street corner for about an hour. He doesn't think we should talk at all anymore. It should be like we are starting new lives. We need to let each other go.

I go back with Jason. Why did I resist him all this time? He has what I've thought of as bad qualities, but maybe he's just being realistic, maybe that's just real life. Maybe he's right. All of his amorality, his insistence on the value of social hierarchy, his belief in exclusivity, his capitalism, his snobbishness—all the things that turned me off before gradually begin to seem appealing. Maybe that's just how you have to be in New York. And after the lacklustre summer in Montreal—where all the romance I imagined was gone—I decide it is time to try something new.

In my first year in New York, I was only half-committed to it, like a casual relationship, like it was a city I was just trying on. But as Montreal let me down, New York glistened ahead of me. I realized that I had to embrace it, even with all of its flaws, and I extended the same logic to Jason too. When I first met him, I didn't want to fall in love with him because he looked like the type of guy that everyone falls in love with; it was too predictable. I didn't want to be another guy tripping all over his good looks, his style, his charm. We fought constantly, bickering layered with sexual tension. So when I go back to New York with him this time, he insinuates that we should date, that we should just fuck all the time, raw. He tells me that he likes me as "more than a friend." I tell him that I like him as more than a friend too but that I don't have romantic feelings for him.

He's been gone for an entire weekend—no parties, no dinners, no text messages from him demanding that I come hang out, no waking up in his shoebox of a bedroom watching him shirtless in the kitchen while I have interesting conversations with Sofia about the Situationists. It stuns me how much I miss him. Finally I see him underneath the arches at Washington Square Park near NYU. As I walk up to him, we smile at each other, and fuck it, maybe I do feel different. I give him a huge hug, gripping him tight. He hugs back and has a surprised look on his face.

"Whoa. What's gotten into you?"

"I don't know. I missed you the whole time you were gone. I was bored. New York is boring without you."

"Uh-huh," he says with a smirk.

After a few errands, I have to go to class. On my way there, I text him to wish him a good day.

"Um ... thanks?" he replies. Then, "You're acting weird."

"I have this crazy idea, Jason," I write. "I want to see what will happen if we start being nice to each other."

"Oh ... okay :) You have a good day too."

I am pretty sure that if we start being nice to each other, we'll just fall in love—it should be as simple as that. He's wanted to be with me this whole time, so it shouldn't be too complicated.

*

I pack up all of Jeremy's things that I still have and put them into a box. I have socks, sweaters, and shirts that were his, but over the course of years, became mine. I have photos of when we were together—it's surreal how young we looked, how in love we were. There's a photo booth snapshot from Montreal. I remember the day clearly. We saw a movie and afterward took the photos. I have a big smile on my face, and Jeremy's drinking a soda. In the next photo, his mouth is open, all gaping wet and pink. In the next, both of us are in profile and my thumb caresses his jawline in mid-kiss, eyes closed, a promise ring on my finger.

I put the photo strips into the box along with the clothes. I bury my face in his clothes, convinced they still smell like him. I mention this to Jason, who tells me that's impossible. The other photos I put in the box are even older, from when we first met. I feel like an asshole and know that I will miss having them; I feel like I am removing my vital organs and putting them into this fucking box. The other photos were cherished, bent at the edges from being in my wallet for so long. One is his high-school graduation photo. His skin looks perfect, his hair is blond, he has a big smile on his face. I think of the last time I saw Jeremy in Montreal, and he doesn't look like this anymore. Now he has a septum piercing and facial hair, and it looks totally ridiculous on him. My boy—with facial hair. Preposterous. The other photo I love even more. It's super old and even more faded. It's a photo of him as a little boy, maybe six or seven years old. I kept it in my wallet as well. It is quintessential Jeremy. He's wearing a red plaid shirt, looking totally Quebecois *pure-laine* (old French-Canadian stock), with a big goofy grin, reddish hair, big ears, the sweetest, most innocent smile imaginable. Who knew such a little angel would be such a heartbreaker? The last thing I place in the box is a pink plastic ball, one that fell from the overhead decorations during the Montreal Aires Libres. I tape the box shut, write his address on it, and then, over the slit where it will be opened, I write the word *nous*. When he cuts the box open, *nous* will become *no us*. Just one little last bit of poetry for him.

I take the box to the post office. Jason tells me that this is a bad idea.

"It's romantic," I say. "Poetic."

He tells me I should throw it all in the trash.

"You have absolutely no respect for the poetry in life," I tell him. "It's a final tragic gesture. I'm not going to take years of involvement with somebody and just throw their shit in the trash. That's what people like you do, and I think that's even more sad than this."

*

I feel better after I send the package. If Jeremy wants it to be done, now it is really done. I focus on Jason, which is weird. He's stopped the relentless pursuit that he started in the spring. Now that I'm not resisting him, he's resisting me. It's as if I take all of my feelings for Jeremy and place them onto Jason. I know this is dangerous. We spend a lot of time together, but I'm not letting him know how I feel yet.

Part of the problem is that when he came to see me in Montreal, he met a guy there. He was staying with me that weekend, but he had grindr open, and the guy messaged him. I knew this guy, Lucas, so I said, "Yes, he's sweet, it's hot, go have fun." But then I admitted, "I feel weirdly jealous about this." I was only half-serious, and Jason just laughed and said, "Later, pseudo-boyfriend."

Now, back in New York, I'm annoyed that Jason keeps going away for a weekend here, a weekend there, to see Lucas. When he comes back, I start to get honest and say, "Hey, remember before I left for the summer, how you wanted to be with me?"

"Arthur. You're crazy. I'm crazy. Well, you make me crazy. It would never work."

"But Jason, admit it: the reason I make you crazy is because you are in love with me. And we've never admitted it to each other or knew what to do about it."

*

I'm driving uptown with Jason in the back of a yellow cab. He's going to see two clients in a row while I wait at a café. In the back of the cab he pulls his dick out and starts to jerk off. He wants the cab driver to see, wants to get caught; it turns him on. When people do weird and crazy things all the time, it starts to seem normal. This is just part of hanging out with Jason. After he sees the clients, we go back to his place, where he takes a shower. I've told myself that I would never let him fuck me after he sees a client, but, I rationalize, he's just taken a shower. He puts his arms around me and we kiss. The taste of his spit is the same as it was last spring, when I didn't care, but I like that something feels the same as it did before, so I let him fuck me.

I start to spend the night regularly again. Jason tells Sofia that I have a crush on him, which is true, and Sofia says, "It is a horrible idea for you to want him. He only fucks people for validation, conquest. He's a narcissist, a player."

"Yeah, I know all of that, but if we just stop picking fights with each other and competing with each other, it'll be fine. And besides, he was crazy about me before."

"But now he knows you want him, so it won't be the same."

Jason smirks. But the sleepovers are nice. He's making enough money as an escort that we can always afford to go out and have drinks or dinner. I try not to think about it. It's easier that way.

*

Jason is tricking in a building across the street, and I'm writing in a café, and I figure that people have been doing this in New York and across the world for decades—we just don't look down-and-out. Now it's all moved online, gone digital.

*

Sofia gives me a black leather jacket. It fits me like a glove. It's the only jacket I wear now. I feel wrapped up in the New York night whenever I wear it.

*

I haven't told Jason yet that I'm starting to have feelings for him or that I finally realize I've had feelings for him the whole time and just denied them or that maybe I'm just transferring all of my feelings for Jeremy onto him, but I think he is starting to become keenly, manipulatively aware of it. One night, we go out for drinks, and he lets me sit on his lap in front of everyone.

"Isn't this a little couple-y?" I ask.

"Come on, you know you're my boy."

And I take that at face value.

So every time we fuck lately—me on my back, my legs wrapped around his shoulders—I don't cum until he cums, and he shoves his thumb between my teeth while he fucks me and calls me a good boy or a bad boy, depending on how I've been behaving lately. I've now slowly trained him how to kiss while he fucks, which he isn't used to. You can tell if someone has never been in love before if they're amazing in bed but can't French kiss worth a damn. But I teach him. While he's fucking me, I put my arm around the back of his head, pull him in closer until our foreheads are touching, and kiss him while he pounds me. He's so taken away by it all, not used to doing both at once, but I tell him with my touch that it's okay. Intimacy is okay.

*

Jason and I walk around the Lower East Side. He takes little cheap shots at me, and we start to wrestle. He thinks it's cute. He swings his arm back and knocks the wind out of me. I lean over, but once I catch my breath, I say, "I'm not a fucking toy. You did that in Montreal a few weeks ago, remember? Fucking knock it off!" He just laughs.

"Look, Arthur, I like to roughhouse. If you can't handle it, I'll just have to find someone stronger."

"I am strong," I say. "That's not the point. I don't do that kind of thing to you. Just cool it down, okay?"

Later, at his apartment, he punches me in the arm.

Sofia says, "You boys need to fucking cut it out before someone gets hurt."

"Oh please. He likes it. I bet he thinks about it when he jerks off, don't you, Arthur?"

I do like how much rougher he is than me, how much tougher, stronger. All of that energy, that physicality, translates to really hot sex. But outside the bedroom, it's as if he doesn't realize that I am a real person. He starts to remind me of one of those demented little children who torture puppies and can't translate their pain but instead are fascinated with the details of the kill. When Jason playfully beats up on me, he just laughs. It is mostly innocent, boyish and fraternal, so I can't get too upset, except when I tell him he's gone too far and he still doesn't seem to care. He thinks it is all part of our game, just like at the boutique, *You be a good little cleaner boy and do what I say otherwise I'll have to punish you.* It's not that hot when he acts like I'm actually his little boy-toy fuck-thing. When the roles aren't play.

*

I can tell that it's working and that he's coming around. After he cums inside me and all the electricity is over, I spend the night, and we cuddle the way boyfriends cuddle. It's not casual cuddling. It's falling-asleep-naked-for-eight-hours-in-a-sweaty-mess cuddling. It is sexy as fuck. It is also, maybe, scary.

*

I'm at a warehouse party when I get a text from Jason: "you wouldn't believe this cute boy I have in my bed." I haven't told him outright yet that I want to be his boyfriend so I don't get pissed. I'm also aware that this is an invitation. He sends me a photo of the boy, a dancer, eighteen but looks about fifteen, with curly brown hair and a tight slender body. Total twink. Jason tells me he's been fucking the boy and breaking him in. He invites me over under the pretense that I'm not allowed to fuck the boy, thinking he's just going to show off in front of me. Clearly, he doesn't know who he's dealing with.

So I take the train across the East River to get there. They're watching cartoons, hanging out in their boxers, just like Jason and I used to do. I crawl into bed with them. Jason closes the laptop, and we all lie down to go to sleep. Before I know it, I hear kissing noises. Jason's in the middle, wanting to fuck the boy in front of me while I do nothing. He's invited me over just to frustrate me, to show me he has options, he can get anyone he wants. A little trick, a little competition. He's on his knees, fucking the boy's face.

"Am I a part of this or not?" I say, to which the boy, much to Jason's surprise, smiles and turns over and starts to kiss and caress me, to stroke my cock. I can see by the look in Jason's eyes that his plan has gone unexpectedly awry. So we share the boy. Jason pushes my head down onto the boy's cock while he continues to fuck his mouth. I start to lick his balls. The kid makes angelic moaning noises that drive both of us crazy. Jason tells the kid to roll over onto his stomach. He spreads the boy's ass cheeks apart and starts to finger fuck his asshole, then he takes his finger and shoves it in my mouth, letting me taste it.

"Get him nice and wet before I fuck him," Jason commands, so I lean down and start to rim the boy's smooth ass, his hole pink and tight, and the kid moans with pleasure as my tongue presses deep into his hole.

Jason pushes me away, climbs on top of the boy, slowly pushes his dick inside him, and starts to fuck him hard, covering his mouth with his hand. I look at Jason and think, *Holy shit, this kid is seriously young, and you should really use a condom or something. This kid has no idea what he's doing.* Jason looks back at me as if to say, *Shut the fuck up.* After pounding the boy's ass and cumming inside him, Jason pulls out and catches his breath on the side of the bed. At this point I'm getting bored, and sort of pissed at Jason for thinking he can make me come all the way here just so that he can fuck some kid in front of me—like the kid won't want me too, like we're not on the same level. Just to piss Jason off, I say to the kid in my bad-boy tone, "Don't you want to try to take my thick cock next?" And the kid looks at my cock and sees that it is considerably thicker than Jason's. He smiles and says "Uh-huh." So I lift his legs up in the air and start to push into his ass, tight and warm, and I thrust a few times before Jason gets jealous and says, "enough," and then kicks me out—"just because."

*

The next day, I ask Jason what the problem was, and he says that the boy wasn't supposed to let me fuck him, that he was supposed to be all for him; the boy disappointed Jason by letting me fuck him. Jason says he was going to date the boy, but decided—after the boy let me fuck him—that he wasn't worth it.

*

I go over to Jason's place after classes. He asks me if I feel like going out, and I say no, not tonight.

127

"Well, I bought some really nice whiskey, so we can at least have a drink, right?"

I accept the offer. He asks me how my classes were as he mixes whiskey and cola. Sofia isn't home, and he's being oddly nice.

"Do you have anything to do tomorrow, any classes, anything important?" he asks.

"No, not really, I just need to read a lot, probably work on a paper."

"That's good. Are you sure you don't want to go out? I mean, considering all the MDMA you just drank, and all?"

I look down into the glass, see the residue.

"Are you fucking serious?" I ask, "You're joking, right? Are you out of your mind? You know I hate uppers, Jason, they give me crazy anxiety. I fucking hate MDMA. I told you I never wanted to do it again. You know that."

"Look," he says, laughing, "it's just my way of apologizing to you for all the shit we've been through lately. This will make us open up, take our guards down, and bond. Like brothers."

"Fuck you," I say.

"You'll calm down once it kicks in," he says. "It's really good stuff. Look, I felt bad for the threesome, for the way I've been treating you, and for kicking you out whenever I felt like being vindictive."

"So in order to repay me, you fucking roofie me?" I say. "I should ... I should call the police on you." By now my heart is racing. "I should go to the hospital."

"You should calm down, Arthur. It's going to hit you either way. You might as well come out with me and enjoy it. Besides, you just said you have nothing to do tomorrow."

"Just because I have nothing to do tomorrow doesn't mean I want to be high as fuck all night and feel like shit for two days after!" I yell. I start pacing, looking for my coat. The last time I did MDMA with Jason, we talked to some stupid fashion design student at his apartment along with some coked-up Russian girl, then we all went to a dance club and watched people vogue. I spilled my guts to Jason while we walked around. We talked about losing our virginity, our ideal lovers, our childhoods—things you shouldn't tell someone you're sleeping with. I didn't want to repeat that. I decided then that I wouldn't do MDMA again.

"I'm too old for this shit," I mutter.

"What are you gonna do? Go home and roll around in your bed? You're gonna be blitzed as fuck either way."

"Fuck you, fuck you, fuck you," I say. "I'm gonna have a panic attack."

He comes over and gives me a hug. "It's gonna be fine. Just go with it."

In order to calm down, I play a mental trick on myself. First, I tell him, no sex after, and he promises, no sex.

"Because then I will really feel like you are date-raping me and taking advantage of me."

No sex. We pinky-swear on it. I tell myself that Jason is really good-looking. We've fucked dozens of times. He is harmless. This is just a little practical joke, it's funny, we're young, it's harmless.

"Why didn't you just ask me if I would do it with you?"

"Because I knew that you would say no," he says.

I tell myself, *Sure, it's against my will, but it's not a big deal. It'll go away. We'll have a good night. He'll keep an eye on me like he always does. I've done this plenty of times before.* Never mind that I told myself I would never do it again. Never mind that he just disregarded my autonomy. *It'll be easier if I just go with it,* I tell myself. *I hang out with crazy people. I know this. I hang out with drug addicts, queers, prostitutes, poets, and pornographers. I've chosen this life. This type of thing is bound to happen. It's bound to happen if you want to feel everything, if you want to see the best and the worst. If I told anyone what was going on, they wouldn't think it was a big deal; they would say, oh, you kids ...* It doesn't occur to me that this is a creeping, gradual form of abuse. Not the torrid love-affair kind that I'm used to, but actual abuse.

I decide that the only way to make him feel like he has not totally fucked me over is to calm down and "go with it." Even though in the back of my head I'm thinking, *Shit, your only "friend" here, your "lover," just spiked your drink.*

And then it starts to kick in, and I succumb. "Well, it is pretty good," I say. I go from zero to ten, rolling, gnawing on the inside of my cheeks. I hate it. My heart can't handle how fast it is beating, but I don't say any of this, I don't want him to know. And there's no one around to tell me how fucked-up this is. Jason makes fun of me when we walk to the bar, but I'm too high to care. When we get there, he even tells people what's going on, and they laugh, sort of nervously. I get into a stupid conversation with a rich old man. Jason keeps telling dumb stories. "Did I ever tell you about the time when..." It might be the first time that I see how totally narcissistic he is, but, then again, I'm really high.

We walk to a club with two guys, friends of Jason's, who are also fucked up. One of them is wearing huge contacts and I ask them why they are so big. He tells me that they're fake, and that he wears them all the time so that people can't tell when he is rolling, because he is always high. At the club, I'm high as fuck—it's all so stupid and everyone around me is so arrogant and rich, it's disgusting. Doing MDMA in Montreal never felt this way, but in NYC it feels awful. Reptilian mind. I cling to Jason. I stare at straight men in their designer suits. Jason tells me that if I want to keep fucking cute boys when I'm older, I have to look like them, I have to start working out, think of longevity.

We stand in the VIP section because Jason knows the host, of course, but he goes downstairs to do some coke with her, telling me very sternly, "Stay here, don't move." I'm so high that it doesn't dawn on me that if I were to move, I could just call him, but not moving and staying put seems like an imperative. Must wait. Must wait for the return of Jason and blond trans host.

As I wait, blitzed out, some average-looking hostess comes up to me, dressed really New Jersey, and tells me that I have to move. I try to be very nice, try to project good vibrations. I tell her that my friend just went downstairs with one of the hosts and told me to meet them back here—they'll be back any minute—and if I move, I'll lose them. She says that she is going to come back in ten minutes with security, so I should be gone by then, because people paid thousands of dollars for these tables. Jason comes back up a bit later, buys me a drink, and luckily the MDMA's wearing off a bit. We go back to his place and watch cartoons. He cuddles me. We don't fuck, he can't get hard anyway. I don't say anything to him about the night, about how fucked-up I think it was to spike my drink, because part of me still believes it's just good fun.

Nothing, no one makes any sense anymore.

*

"Get off. I'm serious, I'd rather leave."

"Nuh-uh."

"Let me go."

"What are you going to do about it?"

"Your roommate is home. I'm tired of this bullshit, now get off me. I said I have to go. What are you going to do?"

"I can do whatever I want."

"Oh, you think that's hot? Get real. Don't make me yell for your roommate."

He gets off of me, slightly, enough to turn me from my back to my side.

"I'm serious," I say, squirming. He starts to unbuckle my jeans, trying to pull them down. I'm not even remotely turned on. He spits on his fingers, trying to get me wet. I yell out, "Sofia! Jason won't get the fuck off of me!" and suddenly he snaps back, pushes me off the bed.

"Fine, then. Get the fuck out," he says.

"I've been trying to."

"I could have done it if I wanted to, by the way," he says as I leave.

*

All this foolishness. Dreams of highbrow domesticity that could rarely come through with you. Through with you. All your affectionate machismo. Narcotic narcissismo. You said love is war. Think you're just a fascist. Spilling my guts all over the Lower East Side.

*

At a fancy cocktail bar where millionaires and trust fund kids are scattered about, Jason disappears into the bathroom now and again with European boys to do lines. He's been doing a lot of coke lately, but he doesn't pressure me to do it with him so I don't care. At the bar, he buys me drinks. People see the way we talk to each other in a coded language, like a couple. Jason and I debate which of two boys we'd rather have a threesome with. I tell him I'm not particularly attracted to either—one with foxy red hair, the other an Italian boy with dark olive skin and black hair. Jason tells me I'm just not drunk enough yet, so he keeps buying me whiskey sodas, and I keep drinking them. I tell him his sex drive is out of control, and it is truly insatiable. We fuck so intensely that I need to go outside after and walk around, collect myself. I wonder where his horniness comes from. We're the same age, and I'm horny too, but for him it's like something else, like a void that he constantly needs to fill with new conquests.

He brings me back to his place. I lie down to go to sleep and tell him that I'm not horny, that I'm drunk and just want to go to sleep. He says "fine, then" and tells me that the Italian boy is coming over.

"Whatever," I say. I'm lying in bed on the verge of sleep when the Italian boy arrives and without exchanging a word, unbuckles his belt, takes off his shirt, and starts to make out with Jason. Instantly their horniness rubs off on me. They're grinding against each other, and all of our dicks are hard. The smell of young men fills the room, the smell of ass and dick and balls and body odour. I'm suddenly more awake. Jason tries to fuck the Italian kid, but he says he's a top, so Jason gets on his hands and knees and the boy, who has an eight-and-a-half-inch thick uncut cock, spits on it and then slowly eases it into Jason's asshole. Jason arches his back and takes it into him without making a sound. I'm on my knees next to the Italian while he fucks Jason, playing with his Italian asshole, jerking myself off, whispering into the Italian boy's ear, "Fuck his hot ass, man, that's it." In the back of my head, I'm thinking, *What the fuck, we never use condoms*, but I'm focused on the Italian boy ramming Jason's ass, pondering why Jason doesn't moan or make any noise when he's getting fucked. He just disappears. I try to touch Jason while he's being fucked, but he pushes my hand away. I want to shove my dick in Jason's mouth while the Italian boy fucks him.

As if he's suddenly run out of patience with the passive role, Jason scoots off the boy's cock and pushes my drunk ass onto the bed—my cue to do whatever he says when he manhandles me like that. I lie on my back. Jason instructs the Italian boy very sternly to sit on my face. He crawls on top of me, parks his asshole right in my face, and starts to grind my face with his ass, his knees beside my chest.

"Just sit on his face and make him shut the fuck up. Suffocate him with your ass," Jason tells the Italian. The kid rests his ass on my face—which Jason knows I'll love, it's like a gift from him to me—and I rim the kid from underneath, devouring his asshole, the funk and smell of it. While I'm doing this, I can feel fingers going into my ass—everything happens so quickly I can't keep track—and I'm drunk off the sex. I'm still rimming the Italian above me, and I can feel Jason pull my legs out a bit, hoisting them up. He quickly sticks his cock in me while the kid grinds my face with his hole. Jason fills me with his cock while I eat the boy's ass, then the boy lifts off me. Jason pulls out and holds my legs back for the Italian boy to shove his cock in me, but he only gets the tip in before I pull back, coming to, gathering myself, saying, "No, I only let Jason fuck me." The Italian boy doesn't spend the night.

*

Trauma bond me a boy in bondage,
Trauma bondage. Come a little
closer, comatose me comatoser.
Trauma bond me, bondage, bruise
me, come and dose me, comatose
me, candy dose me. Spike me and
fuck me. Behold a bruise. Amiss, a
muse. Calm now comatose calm
now smaller doses hold me closer.

*

Jason and I are basically totally acting out, doing whatever we want. He says things like, "Between the two of us we can get any boy in New York."

But I want to move in with him again, damn it. I want a dog, I want to hold hands again and walk around his neighbourhood like we did when I first moved here, and maybe only do this crazy shit once in a while.

Jason tries to carry out a plan that he has devised, I think, to totally corrupt me, to break me into the kind of reckless New York decadence that I missed out on last year. I think of one of the very first things he ever said to me: "You're such a sensitive boy. I'll have to teach you to stop caring." I try to comply, because the deeper I get into his weird world, the more I fall for him and admire his insanity, his total disregard for decency. He reminds me of Jeremy and, in a way, of myself. In his tender moments, there is goofiness, innocence, and strange and rare forms of intimacy.

Jason tells me that he is going to turn a trick and that I should come with him. He knows I'm between jobs and broke right now, so it's an opportune time to introduce me to the world of escorting. I'm uncertain, so he tells me to do it for the story, the experience, the poetry—do it because I'll know him better afterward, it'll bring us closer together. Isn't that what I want? So I go with him to a hotel near Union Square. In the lobby bar we have a drink and he tries to talk me into it.

"It'll be fine," he reassures me. "I've had this client a few times. He's fine. I go in, I fuck him, you fool around, I try and make him cum as fast as possible, and we both walk out with $250. Let's be real here, Arthur—you're chasing poetry in New York City, and it doesn't exactly pay, does it? So just try it with me. You'll walk out laughing, and you'll know me better after." I feel too paranoid and tell him that I'll wait for him at the bar.

He rolls his eyes. "Whatever. Other guys would do it with me."

The bartender eyes me as Jason walks away. I ask for another drink. I imagine how it would go down if I were in the elevator with him right now. Jason would lead the way as we went up to the room and knocked on the door. I would tell Jason to introduce me as Patrick, the name of the eighteen-year-old boy we practically fucked inside-out the other night. I would feel a slight sense of relief if the client wasn't particularly unattractive, just your average guy in his fifties, five-foot-ten, not totally overweight but not in shape either. His demeanour would be nice, not creepy. Jason always described his tricks as "slightly sad, slightly older men who pay me to fuck them."

"Do you like it?" I would ask him in bed.

"Yeah. I like that they want me so badly, they're willing to pay for it. They're so pathetic. That gets me hard. And the money gets me hard."

But then, whenever he had a gig and didn't need to do it for a while, I would say, "I thought you liked it."

Then Jason would grimace and say, "Are you fucking kidding me? It's fucking disgusting. And I feel disgusting about myself afterward. It's the most basic transaction, it's using someone, and then it's hard to distinguish when you're getting paid and when you're not. It becomes hard to fuck differently. Everything becomes like a performance, a negotiation."

I stir the ice cubes in my whiskey and wonder what he's doing upstairs, what it'd be like, and if I should have gone with him. Would he like me better if I did? I imagine him walking confidently into the room, throwing his shirt off, and dropping his pants to reveal tight red underwear, the very pair I used to sniff and jerk off to while he was in the shower. I'd still be unstrapping my boots, confused and nervous. He would kiss the guy briefly, push him onto the bed, lift his legs up in the air, hopefully put a condom on, and then start to fuck the guy. I would walk over, not sure what to do, lying on the bed, stroking my flaccid dick, trying to get hard. I'd watch Jason fuck this guy and wonder how he managed to get hard. The guy would say things like, "Oh yeah, oh yeah, fuck me, you stud, and tell your friend to bring his dick over here."

At this point, Jason would probably give me a dirty look for lying there and doing nothing. Barely hard, I'd manage to face-fuck the guy, try to focus on the feel of his mouth. Jason would flip him over and start to fuck him from behind. We like to tag-team like that. The guy would be on his knees getting fucked by Jason, blowing me, and blabbering about Jason being such a good top. Then Jason would use the trick he always told me about—to start fucking them really fast after about five minutes, jackhammering the guy while he's on his stomach, pounding away. The guy would cum all over his stomach, then that would be it. He'd collect his little envelope and come downstairs.

We take a cab to the East Village. My comfort with this side of him has made us closer, but without my realizing it, it has also pushed us further apart because this is not the side of him he'd ever want someone else to see. He does want someone else to see it, to know it's there, but suspects that once they have, they will have seen too much to ever love him. I think about how Jason does this all the time, how he might feel bad about it, might take it out on other people, and what it means that he can manage to stay hard for money. We have a few drinks, play metal songs on the jukebox to annoy the other gay guys, then Jason runs off to buy a gram of coke that he'll do later tonight. We walk around the East Village talking intermittently about life philosophy and also nothing at all, he throws twenty dollars at a homeless beggar saying, "Money isn't anything, it's so easy to get and lose." The scent of his $200 cologne makes my knees weaken as it wafts in the autumn air, damning me, fucking with my senses, making me wonder how someone so bad could smell so layered and complex, so fucking *rich*.

It starts by borrowing a jacket laced with geranium,
spices like clove, sandalwood, cinnamon. Masculine,
sophisticated scents. Rare, warm exotic notes, incense,
resinoid, styrax, benzoin for comfort. Mostly musk and spit
that I miss the most, how it'd drip down from your lips
as you press the side of my head against your bed. The spit
and the taste of it. A violent room full of violent moods.
I even miss the grip with which fists would fatten my lips
were I to say something amiss. The way the weight
would hold me down, in my place, the soft taste
of the pillow case. Fingertips tickling my ribs
until I can't breathe. The tip of your dick, the quick
slip without consent, but content in knowing that No
drives you crazy. Sometimes a slap is just a playful slap:
sitting in your lap at the bar drinking whiskey sodas,
then downstairs, Home Sweet Home. I miss the collaterals,
the calm nights, the lack of bipolar episodes, a lover

who isn't addled with coke, molly, opiates, and Adderall.

The ability to look at you and believe you're just a boy from California.

*

In any case, now that he tells me he thinks it's a bad idea, I want to try it even more, just to prove him wrong. Or maybe to prove myself wrong.

One morning, I'm running late for class, and he says, "If you fuck me right now, we're officially boyfriends."

"Oh, yeah? Fine," I say. I pull his pants off, put his legs over my shoulders, and fuck him quickly until he shoots all over his stomach. After, he yells out, "Sofi-aaaaa, Arthur is my bf now," and she says, "Shut up. I don't want to hear from you two boys. Someone gonna get hurt." I kiss him goodbye before I leave.

I spend that night at his apartment, as usual. When we wake up in the morning, he tells me that we are talking too loudly and that we'll wake Sofia up. He's in a pointedly pissy mood—didn't get enough sleep, I guess—with an aggressive look in his sharp blue eyes. He punches me in the arm, boyishly, so I punch him in the arm back, thinking we're just fucking around, wrestling like we do, when he suddenly whips around. He raises his arm up and brings it down with his all his weight into it and punches me in the chest. When he raises his arm to hit me again, I move, but not before his fist connects with my bottom lip. It hurts a little bit, but not as much as I imagined getting punched in the face would; it's more the shock that scares me. This happens in an instant. I put my hand up to my lip, cover my mouth, notice the taste of blood. Jason leaves the bedroom and goes into the kitchen. I sit on the edge of the bed and start to cry, not sure what to do. *("Sorry about the blood in your mouth / I wish it was mine / I couldn't get the boy to kill me, / but I wore his jacket for the longest time.")*

Jason comes back in with a glass of water, stands there like nothing happened.

"What the fuck, Jason. You punched me in the fucking mouth, you asshole." I hold back sobs. For some reason I don't want to cry in front of him. I wipe the tears out of my eyes.

"Oh, come on, boo bear," he says, laughing it off, smiling. He gives me a bear hug, pulling me in tight. "You're overreacting. I'm sorry. You moved—I didn't mean to get you in the mouth."

"Get off me, you fucking asshole." I squirm out of his grasp.

"Well, if you don't wanna be hit, then don't hit me, you cute little fucker," he says.

"I've told you a million times to stop being so rough with me, so fuck you. Fuck this. I'm out of here." I grab what I can of my things and go to school.

A few hours later, I return to grab the rest of my stuff. Jason opens the door and says, "Hey, boyfriend." I glare at him, walk into his room, and gather my things. He stands in front of the door, blocking it.

"I'm really done," I say. "This is too fucking much."

"Arthur, you're throwing a hissy fit."

"You punched me in the mouth and then laughed about it, Jason."

"I guess this means we aren't boyfriends."

"Yeah, that's what it means," I say. "Get out of the way."

He stands there with his arms crossed. "Sure, whatever. Quit being such a pussy. Call me when you get over it."

I flip him off, walk past him, and make my way home.

*

Tells me normal boys don't pass up on all of this. Tells me there are a million better places to stick his dick besides me. Tells me he is VGL. Tells me he knows he is crazy, forgive him, because he loves me. Tells me he doesn't know why he wastes his time with me. Tells me if it weren't for the sex, it wouldn't be worth all the bullshit he puts up with. Gives me a job. Gives me a place to live. Tells me he wants to chain me to the radiator, fuck me raw, and leave me there dripping, legs askew. Tells me I'm more beautiful broken. "I hit you, but you're more beautiful because of it." Sends me a pic of that abusive relationship poster in the subway. Tells me he is sorrier than dirt.

*

Before Matthieu and after Fred, there is an even briefer encounter, so brief you won't even remember his name. After so much time, the damage done blends in with all the others, but this one remains distinct to you for some reason, for the feeling of possibility. You are somewhere between your last year of college and your first year of post-college life. He lasts a few weeks, but it feels like a bigger deal at the time—it is that time when people normally work things out and stay together. But you know it won't be like that because he is just a privileged McGill student originally from Vancouver, and it is bound to end badly. But you don't remind yourself of that until afterward, you think of how he looks, how he looks at you, what might happen.

The first time, you agree to meet him at a bar near his college. When you enter, he stands up to shake your hand, and he's so good-looking that you want to turn around and leave to spare yourself the anxiety. Instead, you stay and drink two beers each. You find out that he's an architecture student, which is hot. He speaks slowly and confidently. He's six-foot-three with broad shoulders and short blond hair—not dirty blond—blue eyes, cheekbones that you could cut yourself on, and an extremely masculine jawline. But it's not just the way he looks that drives you crazy. He is the same age as you. You go back to his apartment and lie down in the bed and start to make out, and for the first time in years, despite all the sex you've had, you start to tremble.

"Why are you shaking?" he asks you.

"Just nervous," you say. You're shaking because you really like this one, but you can't say that.

But it's December and you're young and lonely, so you move way too fast. Both of you delete grindr a week after having met. You slip up and bareback once, which you falsely translate as sexual exclusivity. It happens in the morning when he wakes up with a hangover. You stroke his head to make him feel better, which turns into a massage, which turns into massaging his ass and spreading his cheeks apart and rimming his ripe ass, which tastes and smells so good you want it to be yours forever. You turn him over on his back. He's hard and not too bothered by the hangover now, and what begins as some casual poking turns into the first time you ever fuck someone raw. Your brain is flooded by how much better it feels, and now you want to fuck him raw all the time. Now you think he is your boyfriend.

But it's never that simple. And he's not. The conversation about condoms becomes code for "Are we fucking other people? Are we together or not?" He wants to still use condoms, which you take to mean that either he doesn't trust you or he wants to fuck other people. You try to put it in the back of your mind. He is leaving for Vancouver soon, and you think maybe you'll go with him. You have sleepovers, but he doesn't like to cuddle, says he doesn't like to be touched. This is weird and a red flag, but you don't acknowledge it.

The sleepovers continue. You get used to the way he and his apartment smell like organic soap, that particular fragrance that West Coast boys have. You've been dating for a month or so, and you try to play it cool, but you're a fucking mess. You're in love. It becomes harder to hide. But you think maybe he is too. What evidence do you have? He comes to parties and dances only with you, looks only at you. He gives you a pink T-shirt that doesn't fit him, a vintage kitschy one that reads "Quebec." He tells you that you look gorgeous in it. He plays acoustic music as you wake up and shower in the morning. You lie in his bed thinking that this must be how these things happen. You and he go to a café and afterward, kiss each other goodbye. It becomes okay to randomly show up, to meet for a quick hang out, to stop by between classes with only enough time for him to fuck your mouth and tell you that boys don't cry as your eyes water because you're gagging.

But then, as he prepares to go home for a few weeks, he grows distant. He leaves under the guise that everything is fine but then gives you a call when he's 3,000 miles away and tells you that he isn't sure that he wants a boyfriend. You ask him to be honest; is it just that he doesn't want a boyfriend or that he doesn't want you as a boyfriend? He assures you that it isn't about you.

When he comes back, you hang out one more time, but he doesn't want you to sleep over at his place. You take a cab home and never see him again, never get any answers. Years later, you run into someone at a nightclub who asks about him, tells you he loved him. To be polite, you ask what happened, and the guy says, "Well, he moved back to Vancouver, alone."

*

"I really do just miss you. I have an empty space where you were."

"An empty space is usually what you end up with when you hit something hard enough."

Make mistakes. Make believe. Believe him.

*

I hook up with a straight guy from London. It is hot; every straight guy needs a tongue up his asshole to realize his true potential. And I have been ignoring Jason's calls and texts for a month. I am out at a party on a Tuesday night and someone warns me: Jason is here. Just then, Jason comes up to me, and he's all fucked-up on I don't even know what. He pleads with me: "Listen, I know you hate me, and I'm so sorry I have been such an asshole to you, I don't even blame you for hating me. I'll do anything you say, if you'll please just take me back and talk to me again." He literally gets down on his knees—in the middle of the dance floor and clasps his hands together like he's praying. "I'll do anything you say," he repeats. I look around, embarrassed on his behalf. I wonder why he looks so clammy and sweaty. I can see that he is skinnier. I tell him to get up and pull him up by his arm.

"I don't hate you," I admit.

"You don't?" He picks me up and gives me a giant hug. I run my hand through his sweaty hair and then we kiss. His mouth tastes dry, but it is somehow still sexy. We go into a corner to talk things over. Jason's obliterated, wasted, but looking better than ever.

"I know I was always bad to you, but it's because I hold you in contempt," he says. "You will probably get everything you want and very soon, and you don't even realize it. You'll get a teaching job, you'll get published. I'm jealous of you because you know what the hell you want to do with your life, and I have no idea. So I give you a hard time for it. I know it's wrong, but there you have it."

When I leave the party, I unblock his phone number. He sends me text messages, selfies of himself vomiting, the spit hanging down from his mouth. I wonder how he still manages to look cute. Jason asks me if I love him and says I better answer because he might die anyway, so I say, "Yes, I love you in a complicated way that doesn't quite make sense to me."

He says, "I love you in a simple, complicit way."

The next day, he denies saying all of it and then concedes that it must have been a strategy, a ploy.

*

The next night, I invite him over to reconcile, watch a stupid zombie movie, and "cuddle." I ask him what the fuck the texts meant, why he was vomiting, what was he on, and does he want to be together?

"Hey," he says, "did I come over here to be interviewed or did I come here to watch a movie?" He spoons me, licks his fingers, brushes them over my asshole, and sticks his cock in me. We haven't fucked in over a month, and it feels so good. We both cum, then resume watching the movie. Twenty minutes later, he tries to reposition my body against the wall, our knees on the mattress with him behind me.

"Come on, not again," I say.

Jason wraps his forearm around my neck and says, "Shh." He puts his hand over my mouth. "Shh. Be a good boy." He sticks it in and fucks me like that, drilling me from behind, and cums in me again. I shoot against the white wall. I can't not cum.

As Jason gets dressed, I ask him, "What are we?'

"What we always are—friends with benefits, undefined lovers."

"Give me a fucking break, Jason. Do you remember what you texted me last night?"

"I was fucked up, I was on drugs." He puts his boots on.

I walk him to the door and open it. "I have enough friends," I say, which is not even remotely true. I push him out and slam the door, hearing him stumble backward. I walk to my mattress and fall into it, feeling fucked out, not caring. Fifteen minutes later, I get a text message that says: "okay fine maybe more than friends but we have to take it easy. you really have the worst timing because there's another boy in the picture."

*

And then, before the other guy comes back, Jason texts me at two a.m., and I agree to meet him at a bar. We play a game of pool while his friends watch. It's all pretense. I get in a cab and go back to Manhattan with him. We walk around the West Village, then go to an apartment that an out-of-town friend asked him to take care of. He draws a hot bubble bath. The apartment is gorgeous, luxurious. We get naked and drunkenly step into the hot water. I'm so drunk I can hardly talk. He splashes water at me, and we spit water at each other, flick clouds of bubbles at each other, little cloud nines. I'm drunk and tired, on the verge of passing out. Jason pulls the plug on the bath and the water drains out. He picks me up out of the tub, dries me off with a towel, and guides me over to the couch in the living room. He lays me down on my stomach. Half awake, I tell him that I don't want to. He fucks me quickly on the couch, dresses me, then we stumble outside. Jason hails a cab back to his place.

In his bedroom, he pins me down and kisses my neck. Tells me to stay the night.

"Jason, what are we doing here? What's the deal—are we in love or not?"

He hesitates a minute, bites his lip. "No," he says.

"Bullshit, because I love you. You're just afraid to say it."

"Is this some kind of trick?"

Drunk and laughing, I say, "No, you dumb motherfucker, this is not a trick. You're a trick! When I met you, you were a prostitute. You just said you don't love me, but I'm saying, regardless, I finally admit it: I love you, even though I shouldn't, even though you don't really deserve it, and it took me all this time to say it. I love you, you fucking, dirty, sexy, crazy mess of a person. And I don't believe you that you don't love me. Why would I be here if you don't?"

"Fine, maybe I do love you ... but you're gonna have to wait for it."

"Why?"

"Because you made me wait for it, and now it's your turn to wait."

"But I didn't know it at the time."

"Doesn't matter. You came back. Now I can do whatever I want."

"I didn't come back, Jason. I let you back in."

"Well, that's a matter of perspective. Look, Arthur, your bad-boy attitude doesn't fool me. I know you care about what I'm about to say, for once. I know you care because everyone hates it when it's not their choice. I know you care because I can feel your heart is racing, even through the blanket. So my answer is the same as yours was before: I don't know what I want yet."

"But I didn't make you wait for anything on purpose," I protest. "I just didn't think you were being sincere."

At the time it doesn't dawn on me that maybe he doesn't know how to love either way, so I accept it. We fall asleep there, his arms wrapped around me.

*

I decide to go to Montreal over the holidays to be alone and write for a few days. Jason tries to make me feel guilty about this, saying, "Sure, run away from me again like you always do." And as soon as I get there, I text Jeremy: "I'm in Montreal."

"Come over," he responds. When I arrive, he is home alone. He looks the same as ever. I feel like I'm cheating on Jason but decide not to worry about it because we aren't official. Jeremy feels like he is cheating on Antoine because he is. We talk for a little while about the people in our lives, feeling the growing distance between us.

"I thought we weren't supposed to talk anymore, after this summer and all," I said to him.

"Antoine and I are in a weird place right now so it's okay. Plus, I'm really horny."

We lie down on the bed and start to make out. I go down on him, eat him out, and he brings my cock up to his mouth and pretends like he doesn't want to suck it. He says, "No, sir, I don't wanna." At first I'm puzzled, and then I remember and play along, but it doesn't work. I don't feeling like owning him. He isn't driving me crazy. But I flip him over and rim his ass anyway, because I love it so much. After a while, we both cum—but at different times—and we lie there in silence.

"Hmm," I say.

"That ... wasn't very good."

"I know," I say. "I don't understand. We never have sex that isn't good."

"It's changed. Wow."

"What?"

"You're not in love with me anymore. It's gone."

"I'm just used to it with Jason, that's all," I say. "I haven't taken charge in a while. And yeah, I'm in love with him."

We hang out a little longer. I want to watch a movie with him and spend the night and cuddle, like when we were kids, but he won't let me. He gives me a few of his Adderalls and tells me to go and write.

It's the last time I see him in person for several years.

*

Laid out like
a butcher's map

Lovers cross the boundaries
of your heart and body

A goosestep waltz, hand over fist
Just a man following orders

Just another fascist soldier
Marching past a border

*

Jason asks me to come back from Montreal earlier than I had planned, suggesting that we could spend a few days together before his other prospect gets back. Since I feel guilty about seeing Jeremy in Montreal, I agree to go back early.

It is snowing lightly in the West Village. I've never seen the city so deserted before. I go up to Jason's place and ring the buzzer. At the door to his room, he greets me, shirt off, but he's acting bizarre.

He tells me to put my book bag down outside his room. After a few minutes of small talk in his bed, he jumps up toward me and starts to run his hands through my hair.

"You have fleas."

"Jason, what are you talking about? Get off me."

"Yeah, huh, you're a dirty Brooklynite hipster who just got back from Montreal. I started to feel itchy as soon as you got in my bed."

He starts to frantically peer at the bed, running his hands over the sheets, brushing away imaginary fleas. He peers at the clothes I'm wearing, scratches his thighs and arms. He's convinced I've brought fleas into his room.

"Have you ever had fleas before? I had them once, and we had had to throw out all the furniture. I will not have them again!"

"Would you please stop it? I don't have fleas, asshole, and you're acting weird."

He scowls at me. "You can stay, but take your shirt and pants off just in case."

After he calms down, we get back into bed and lie there for about five minutes before his boner, which pokes against me, slides out of his boxers. We fuck twice and then he falls sleep. When he wakes up, he's sweaty and says he doesn't want to be touched. Later I realize that he's been snorting heroin.

*

I am in his bed, yet again, and he decides that I cannot leave. He pins me down. I tell him that I really need to go. I have to get dressed; I have a class to go to.

"Go ahead and try to move."

"Jason, would you fuck off? I'm going to be late, let me go." I try to get up but he squeezes my arm, forcing me down. Then he lets go, but he still straddles me, his knees pressed into my shoulders. I try to sit up and he punches me in the arm, hard.

"What the fuck," I say, lunging at him with both arms. He grabs me by the wrists and pins both of them down, then repositions and puts both of his hands around my biceps again.

"Stop trying to move. Stop struggling," he says, grinning now.

"Get off!" I squirm up and down, but the more I move upward or to the side, the harder he grabs my arm.

"Okay." I lie down, panting. "You win, big bro. Fat ass."

"Watch it, lil bro. Wouldn't want to see what I can do when I'm upset. Maybe next time I won't actually let you go."

He gets off me and I leave. Two days later, I find bruises on both arms. Clouds of bruises. *A blue-black bruise from a muse like you.* I wear long-sleeved shirts the rest of the week.

*

During that winter, I watch you do coke in bed. You try to shove it up my asshole. You say that you want to make me feel numb for once. I say, "Feeling numb is your job." We make out on the roof of the Standard Hotel in the dead of winter. You threaten to kill me if I tell the other boy, tell him everything.

*

Everything starts to blur, and it becomes hard to keep track of. What day was this story told or this lie, and what was true and what wasn't? When was he being serious, when not? When was he high? When was it manipulation, when honesty? There are stories that wrap around my head in different directions. Like this one:

"Have you ever been to Coney Island? You can fuck some real young boys there."

"How young?"

"He was in the bathroom at Coney Island. You know, a kid. Watching me pee. I showed it to him. We went into the stalls. He was crying."

"Why was he crying?"

"It was messy, you know. He was embarrassed."

"How young was he, Jason?"

"I don't know, *young*. He was a little kid."

"You mean like a teenager, right?"

"No," he says, laughing. "But he wanted it."

And then there is the time when we're on the bus to Jersey, and he yanks his dick out like he did in the back of a taxi cab once. He tells me that he fucked a fifteen-year-old on this bus. Maybe it's true. And when he kicks me out of his apartment again for not wanting to fuck, says "Why do you think you're here if not to fuck" maybe it's true, when someone else who used to be friends with him tells me all the things he did. You think, *Maybe it's true, that story about a police report that got called off, a set of stairs, and him plunging a sharp object into the guts of another lover.* He tells me that he was falsely diagnosed with schizophrenic personality disorder when he was a teenager. Maybe it's true.

*

What is left in all this leaving? You alone there, in the evening. Your cheekbones will not save you. The open bar will not save you, darling. You have some other holes to rape. Go return your videotapes. In another time, another place, I miss the way your asshole tastes. You say assholes smell like dead cockroaches. I say they smell like cinnamon. In the New York tenements, teach me all your discipline. I'm all bloody, insulin, as I pin you down, my friend.

Says chill and be cute, be cool. Says you had your chance last year, now be a good boy and wait. Spits in your face when he is sick to try to make you sick too. Says stop making yourself into a victim; no one will ever believe you anyway— statute of limitations, hon, haven't you heard of it? Show him the photos on your phone of the bruises on your arms. All he can say is, "Well, you got those because you were moving. It's your own fault for resisting. I can't help it if you bruise so easily." Says you resonate more than other guys. Says you're crazy and you make him crazy. That we're like oil and water. That I really have a hold on him. Do I think he would be doing this if he didn't care, if it was only sexual? Says we both look very young. We can get away with all of this craziness for as long as we damn well please. Says I have the kind of beauty that grows on people. Apologizes for accusing me of having fleas. Says he was on a lot of heroin over the winter. Says sorry. Says sorry. Says sorry. Says a lot of interesting things. Calls me a slut when he fucks me. Fuck that's hot. His own personal cum dumpster, "as opposed to impersonal?" We laugh, calls me a dirty little pervert when he fucks me, a bad boy when he fucks me. I am a fucking bad boy.

*

There is a period of time when we are not supposed to do this type of thing anymore. One night, we try to go to bed without having sex with each other.

"So that's it?" I say. "We can't even touch each other anymore?" It feels foreign. He sighs and rolls over, puts his arm around me.

"This is stupid. This sucks. I know I'm the one who blew you off before but ..."

Soon the cuddling turns into him on top of me. We kiss each other, then he pulls my legs up and fucks me. There is anger and delayed passion in the sex. He leans down and kisses me. "Fuck me, dude," I say, breathless, then I cum on my stomach while he cums inside me. Afterward, we fall asleep next to each other. He holds me all night, and it is like I have broken through to some other person, some younger version of Jason, someone I rarely ever see but who I like so much that I keep waiting around for him to reappear.

*

"Technically, you're cheating on him. Or me, if you take the long view," I say.

"You just have to be patient."

"He's stupid and you know it. I don't care if you're not with me, but you should at least not debase yourself by being with someone so intellectually challenged just because you think he's good looking."

"So what if he's stupid?" Jason says, laughing. "And anyway, I never really cheated on anyone. Humans can never really touch each other."

"What are you talking about?"

He sits up, opens his laptop, and finds a YouTube video that he's clearly watched before. It's a scientific video that shows how, at a sub-atomic level, two objects can never really touch each other.

He looks at me, smiling.

"That's the most depressing thing I've ever seen," I tell him, rolling over and going to sleep.

*

I meet Jason at a café where he makes a grand, sweeping apology. He clasps both of my hands and promises that things will change, tells me I'm the only one who matters, that he was scared and nervous, and that we should move in together soon. I'm skeptical, and it makes me notice little things, the way he can feign a posh wannabe-European upper-class lilt when he wants to sound sophisticated despite probably only having a GED and coming from a poor background. But my skepticism does nothing to dampen my horniness or desire—it never has. We walk back to his apartment.

I try to say something reasonable: "You've been fucking me around this entire time, on and off, and now you say—" But then he just rolls his eyes, grabs me by the shirt, and pushes me against the wall with his tongue down my throat. He can tell that I barely believe him, but he still manages to get my dick hard. Then he pulls down my pants and starts to straddle my cock, slowly sitting down on it.

"Come on, Arthur. I'm sorry. You know I'm sorry, babe. I need you. I love you, Arthur," he says while he starts to ride it. I decide that he's in for a pounding, so I press him against the wall and fuck him hard, noticing how wide open his asshole is. This is exactly what he wanted, so I pound him, smelling his cleaned-out insides on my shaft, the smell of spit and bowels. I fuck him balls deep, and he keeps saying, "I love you, I love you."

"Don't fucking say that if you don't mean it, Jason."

But he keeps saying it with his hand around my neck while I fuck him, keeps saying it until he cums. Afterward, I half expect him to say, "Just kidding, boo," but he doesn't. We get dressed and go off in different directions. I keep expecting to get a text later that says, "I was just fucking with you," but it doesn't happen.

*

Jason comes back after weeks away over the summer. He sees me at a bar. He spills his guts to me again, how he was terrified, how other things seemed easier. Another boy walks into the bar while we are making out, the other fool in the situation, and asks Jason what is going on. Jason tells him he's in love with me, that he must have known this, that they're broken up and he has no reason to be acting so hysterical.

One week later, I see the boy at the bar, but Jason isn't around. I take the boy home and fuck him. We talk about Jason. "He just lies all the time. Who knows who he lies to more?"

*

He pulls me into him when I fuck him, says, "I love you." I feel like I am living inside of a dream, a time warp. We do normal things, go to the gym, have dinner with friends, act like nothing bad ever happened. Manuel, an ex of his from Madrid, is visiting from out of town. We meet him and his girlfriend at a bar. Jason convinces us to go back to his place. There, he brings out the coke, which he cuts up into four huge lines. He offers it to us, but the Spaniards look confused and decline.

"Fuck it," Jason says, and suddenly snorts the four thick lines all at once, one after the other, until all the white powder is gone. He lets out a crazy laugh afterward. We stare blankly at him.

We decide to go to a party, and I ask Manuel, who Jason used to say he was in love with, if he ever had to deal with this kind of behaviour. "I've never seen him that out of control before," he says. "He's not the same person."

Later, I tell Jason that I do love him, but that he really needs to calm down with the drugs.

"I love you too," he says. "Don't worry about me, I'm fine. I know exactly what I'm doing."

After the party, we walk home together, swaying into each other. Outside his apartment, we kiss. "I do really love you," I say again, "but please tone it down."

"You do love me," is all he can say in return, with a big smile on his face. Nothing about the drugs. We go to sleep that night and he's covered in sweat again.

A few days later, he invites a teenager to join us for a threesome. He has bags of coke in his pockets. He doesn't listen to other people. In the morning, I wake up and fuck him. He says, "It hurts." I say, "You want it to hurt." On my way out the door, I leave my keys to his place on the table. I say, "I'll talk to you later."

*

Why can't I find a muse who doesn't fucking destroy me? Jason tells me he's fucked plenty of boys raw when he was fucking me—so no, he doesn't know if he is negative. Says his coke habit is fabulous, merely performance art. Does so much coke he can't stay hard. Says he couldn't talk to me; it took months for him to build up the courage. He can only talk to me now because of the gram that he just snorted in the bathroom. *Darling, I will be the death of you.* Says he only went with the other guy because the guy's mother died; he didn't have any real feelings for him, but he felt bad for him. This suggests he is capable of empathy, which isn't believable.

Says that I come back because I like pain even though I made it perfectly clear that I wanted to play house. Looks at me in the checkout lane while he shoplifts the most expensive cooking oil. Says, "Domestic activities turn you on, huh?" I was only half smiling contentedly to myself. Reads my mind like that. Says I must be real sore about global capitalism not collapsing after all. Pins me down, spits in my mouth, sprays me with Fou d'Absinthe, says it's a good fit for my skin. Smells my neck after having not seen me in three months and says I smell amazing, asks me if I started to shower regularly. I have not showered in three days. Collapses on top of me, says he likes my new gym-boy body. Can't even throw me around the way he used to.

"I gained twenty pounds since last winter," I tell him, "and if you ever hit me again, I will knock you the fuck out and steal all your money."

The hair on his back and shoulders is rivered with sweat, his heart beats dangerously fast, his skin is cold. But despite being dehydrated from the alcohol and drugs, his mouth still manages to taste great.

*

A few weeks later, I get a call from Sofia, his roommate.

"At least it happened when he was still young, dear."

"What are you talking about?"

"Jason. He overdosed. He's dead."

I'm silent.

"Don't act surprised," she says. "We all saw it coming."

"I know, but ..."

"You couldn't have stopped it, darling. You! You are always trying to help people. You get that from your mother. Stop it. He made his choice. It was probably intentional."

"He was trapped in it," I say, dumbfounded, sort of relieved.

"It's more beautiful like this. He would have wound up with some housewife of a boy, balding, bloating, becoming his father. Just like I warned him!" She paused. "Better to go out with a bang. Anyway, I must be the trans angel of death. Transitioning boys to the other side. That jacket he gave you that winter? That belonged to my ex before he jumped off the Williamsburg Bridge. And he tried to wrap you up in it, that bastard. I'm glad you lost it. It had bad energy. Some people weren't made for this world." She starts crying, clearly distraught.

"That might be true," I tell her, "but don't act like they were made for the next, either. If you want to make your heart stop, there are sure-fire ways. You have the choice to feel or not. He made that choice. There are plenty of people who make that choice who just go on living. If you can call it that. I thought maybe he would do that, instead ..."

"You can cut all the flowers, but you cannot keep spring from coming, dear," she says then hangs up.

*

"I think that once you fall in love with someone, you never really fall out of love with them," my friend says. We're out at a rooftop party.

"I think I would have agreed with you a few years ago, but not anymore. You can definitely fall out of love with someone. There are things people can do to make that happen. You can hang on to how you felt about them, or you can move past it."

In mid-conversation, I feel someone tug on my shoulder almost aggressively. I turn my head to see Jeremy standing there. I haven't seen or spoken to him (at his request) for a year and a half.

"Hi," he says, with his big goofy smile. "How are you? Please don't get mad!"

I can hardly believe not only that he's here, but that he had the nerve to approach me after not talking to me for so long. I say, "What are you doing here?"

He explains that he is visiting a friend in New York. I almost don't want to talk to him, but we go off and talk privately. I feel relieved because any sort of attraction for him that I felt before is gone. He doesn't look the same.

"I really thought I'd never see you again," I tell him.

"I know. I wasn't sure either."

"There are some things I need to tell you," I say. "I think it was totally fucked-up that you cut me out completely when I was calling you about something totally unrelated to us. You cut me out at a horrible time. I was in this fucked-up thing. You sort of knew that at the time. I was so deep into it that I couldn't see how bad it was. And I called you. At that point, I wasn't in love with you; I was calling you as a friend. But you still said no. Jeremy, we'd promised that we would never say no to each other. I couldn't believe it. I tried to explain to you that I wasn't calling about us."

"It was one of the worst things I've ever done to someone," he says. "I still feel bad about it. But I had no way to tell that you wouldn't have gone back to focusing all of your attention on me."

"I wouldn't have. I tried to tell you, it wasn't like that. But looking back on it, I can see why you would've thought that. I realized that we shouldn't have tried to be friends in the first place, because I was still way too much in love with you. But you cut me out at the worst time. I'm sorry for the way I acted before. I'm not in love with you anymore and I haven't been for a while. I was just set on this idea of "us." But for the record, I believe that it could have all worked out if you wanted it to. The problem was how you felt about me."

"Hey, I get it. How do you think I feel?" he asks, taking a drag off his cigarette.

"What do you mean?"

"I know that no one is ever going to love me as much as you loved me."

"Good. That's true," I say, with zero hesitation. "And yet ..."

"And yet, I chose to ignore that and keep searching because I always feel like I need more. So in a way, I'm constantly setting myself up for disappointment."

"At least you admit that now. That's not love you're looking for, it's something else."

"I tried the domestic thing with my ex, the one I started to see when you left Montreal. We moved in together. But I would just get crushes on other people, and so would he—sometimes even on the same people. And then he started acting crazy too, bringing guys home for me to discover in our bed. I'm moving out soon anyway. It's over."

"I have to admit, I'm really happy for you."

"Why?"

"Because for a minute there, I was worried that you would become one of them. Another clone. That this wild kid I used to be madly in love with was becoming just another mid-twenties bore, working some boring ass job, settling for mediocrity and some dull, middle-class life."

He stares at me with fire in his eyes. "I can't believe you think I would go down that road."

"Like I said. For a minute. But here you are. Searching someone out at a party. On a weeknight."

Our conversation trails off, and we go downstairs for another drink. I recognize the feeling in my chest; I'm experiencing so many emotions at once that I can't even identify them. I'm glad that can still happen. I say goodbye to my friend and we take a cab back to my place, talking the entire time. He tells me that, even though I was intense, he still knew I would and could never really hurt him. I tell him that, even though he cut me out, I intuitively knew that it wasn't malicious. And that's where a critical difference between people exists, we decide. Do you intentionally hurt people? When you go on adventures—when you're confused, lost, listless, horny, desperate, when you want to feel young forever, when you don't want to give in, when you would rather keep going than lie to yourself—do you intentionally hurt people in the process? Can you own up to your behaviour? Can you still be friends?

I explain to Jeremy that I moved into my place in Brooklyn after we quit talking, after a big fallout with Jason just before he overdosed, after my job contracts dried up, and I had hardly any money while finishing graduate school. It was no longer fun, no longer felt youthful and punk. But things actually turned out for the best: I went from unemployed to finally finding a good job. I tell him that I understand that boundaries are necessary for us to be friends again. I think I learned that the hard way.

As the conversation slows down, the night wears on, and we decide to make that same mistake we always do. Now, there's no sentimental feeling involved, no sense of longing. Afterward, I still feel compelled to ask him if he thinks it will be the last time. "Probably not," he says. And it isn't.

We stay up until the morning, until he has to leave to take the bus back to Montreal. He says we should ease back into our friendship, take it slow, talk only once in a while. I watch him from my window until he disappears out of sight, then go to bed to sleep, still half drunk. I dream that I apologize to him, and in the dream, I can feel him leave me again. I wake up crying, confused, but realize that I actually feel fine. I realize that that initial feeling will always be there, and in a way it's good to know how that feels, to know both sides. It's a way of measuring things.

*

Over the coming weeks, we negotiate, talk more often on the phone, online. For the first time in years, we can talk about other people, other guys, tell each other our stories, and I don't get insanely jealous and he doesn't feel implicated in some way. I notice that he is in the same place I was a few years ago: single when he didn't expect to be, fresh out of love, yearning with desire, confused.

The next time I visit Montreal, we meet up at a bar; another time, I go to his new apartment and we go out together to parties with his new friends. It finally feels possible and normal to know each other. At the party, we hug each other, whiskey flowing into a bit of ketamine, and he says he is glad that we will always be friends, that this is what he always imagined it would be like.

During the embrace, I can feel the difference between us, and I want to point it out to him. He looks different, and he still reinvents himself every year in an effort to find himself. He surrounds himself with new friends at new parties—with all the same drugs. What does it mean that I'm his oldest friend there, and yet I'm the least convinced that he's finally where he wants to be? All those things about him that used to seem so special, I can't find them anymore. They're in a poem somewhere, a memory, but not in front of me. In my head, I want to make corrections, to set the record straight. I compulsively want to ruin the moment with a kind of revision, a reminder of what was. But I don't. I just hug him back. He gives me a little kiss on the cheek. It's an accomplishment, really, that we've managed to make it this far, almost a decade, and still be in that moment together. Even if it doesn't last, that's fine. I think I know the difference now between making the choice to be like this with someone versus choosing not to extend sympathy or forgiveness to them, not wanting to feel everything with someone anymore.

*

You are in a hallway about to leave a party. The colours flash red, blue, black, white, purple. You catch an eye that is a shimmer in a ray of amber. His eyes fix upon yours, adjusting. He is tall, well-built, maybe twenty-five, twenty-six. He has that type of young face that matures well. As you walk past, he catches up with you. He says he's visiting from Berlin. He asks to come home with you.

Because what you didn't get until now is that the story just continues, here or anywhere. The only thing that changes is your perception, your sense of urgency, necessity, finality. You stay aware of those moments of romantic grandiosity while recognizing that they're just moments in a long sequence. You recognize the differences in people, stay friends with those who are true, and can respect yourself more.

You think about the Eric Dolphy quote: "When you hear music, after it's over, it's gone, in the air, you can never capture it again." Life is like that. Love is like that. Which is why you want life to not only be like poetry, but also more like a tattoo—to feel permanent yet somehow still fleeting and ephemeral. But then you have Claude Debussy—"Music is the silence between the notes." The silence between the notes and between people is a part of the music too. It's over, you can never capture it again, but it's all part of a longer piece of music if you keep listening to it, if you train your ear.

You used to think that there was a timeline, that things somehow fit into a sequence, but what you've learned is that time, like love and friendship, isn't actually linear at all. The boys keep coming, and possibilities, rather than narrowing or culminating, only expand. You just have to be aware of it, to be able to feel when something significant is happening. The more you experience, the harder it is to remember how novelty felt in the first place. You can risk confusing chaos for novelty when you're trying to hold on to how it feels when two people meet and time slows down to make you more aware of it. If you teach yourself, you can listen for it.

"Sure," you say to the boy from Berlin. You go into the cab together as strangers. You leave the cab into the night, still strangers, but a little bit less so.

ACKNOWLEDGMENTS

I'd like to thank the following people for their support during the writing of this book. Your individual feedback and encouragement has been paramount. To my mentors, teachers, and editors: Daniel Allen Cox, Sina Queyras, Brian Lam, Kim Freudigman, and Susan Safyan. Thank you.

Nick Comilla was born on a military base turned ghost town in Rome, NY, and grew up in rural Pennsylvania. He is a graduate of the Creative Writing program at Concordia University in Montreal, and completed his MFA in poetry and fiction at The New School in New York. His work has appeared in *Lambda Literary, Poetry Is Dead, Assaracus,* and elsewhere. *Candyass* is his first novel. He lives in New York City.